A Word from Stephanie
about Being a Spy

It all started when our basketball team was revving up to face our biggest rival—Kennedy Middle School. They were counting on our new mascot, Bingo the raccoon, to be at the game.

You see, Allie found Bingo at night on the school grounds, hurt, a few weeks ago. She took him in to take care of him. Ever since then, the basketball team hasn't lost one game. So they consider Bingo their good-luck charm—until this morning, when Allie discovered Bingo was missing from his cage! The basketball team and everyone else in school thinks the kids at Kennedy Middle School mascotnapped Bingo. And stole our good-luck charm! But they don't know how to prove it.

Fortunately, I do! I'm going undercover at Kennedy, posing as a new student. My mission: to spy on the kids there and find out if they have Bingo. But I have to keep my mission top secret if it's going to work. I can't even tell my family! And that's a lot of people to keep a secret from!

In fact, right now there are nine people and a dog living in our house. And for all I know, someone new could move in at any time. There's me, my big sister, D.J., my little sister, Michelle, and my dad, Danny. But that's just the beginning.

When my mom died, Dad needed help. So he asked his old college buddy, Joey Gladstone, and my Uncle Jesse to come live with us, to help take care of me and my sisters.

Back then, Uncle Jesse didn't know much about taking care of three little girls. He was more into rock 'n' roll. Joey didn't know anything about kids, either—but it sure was funny watching him learn!

Having Uncle Jesse and Joey around was like having three dads instead of one! But then something even better happened—Uncle Jesse fell in love. He married Rebecca Donaldson, Dad's co-host on his TV show, *Wake Up, San Francisco*. Aunt Becky's so nice—she's more like a big sister than an aunt.

Next Uncle Jesse and Aunt Becky had twin baby boys. Their names are Nicky and Alex, and they are adorable!

I love being part of a big family. Still, things can get pretty crazy when you live in such a full house!

FULL HOUSE™: Stephanie novels

Available from MINSTREL Books

FULL HOUSE™
Stephanie

My Three Weeks as a Spy

Ellen Steiber

A Parachute Book

Published by POCKET BOOKS
New York   London   Toronto   Sydney   Tokyo   Singapore

A MINSTREL PAPERBACK *Original*

 A Minstrel Book published by
POCKET BOOKS, a division of Simon & Schuster Inc.
1230 Avenue of the Americas, New York, NY 10020

A PARACHUTE PRESS BOOK

 Copyright © and ™ 1998 by Warner Bros.

FULL HOUSE, characters, names and all related indicia are trademarks of Warner Bros. © 1998.

ISBN: 0-671-00832-3

First Minstrel Books printing March 1998

10 9 8 7 6 5 4 3 2 1

A MINSTREL BOOK and colophon are registered trademarks of Simon & Schuster Inc.

Cover photo by Schultz Photography

Printed in the U.S.A.

My Three Weeks as a Spy

CHAPTER

1

◆ ◂ ◂ ◆

"Bingo, you are the cutest little raccoon I've ever seen!" Stephanie Tanner glanced at the gray-and-black raccoon. He sat in his cage on one of the long black tables in the biology lab.

Stephanie pushed a slice of apple through the wires of the cage. "Want this, Bingo?" she asked.

Bingo's round eyes stared up at her first. Then they gazed hungrily at the fruit.

"Careful, Steph," Darcy Powell cautioned. Her chocolate-brown eyes flashed a warning. "Bingo's cute, but no wild animal is ever totally tame. My cousin once got bit by a rabbit that we thought was tame."

"How did that happen?" Allie Taylor asked.

1

Darcy grinned. "He stuck his finger in the rabbit's mouth. He wanted to see if it had teeth. It did. He had to have a whole series of rabies shots."

Stephanie's eyes widened in horror. "I remember now, my dad always tells me to be extra careful around wild animals. Are you sure Bingo won't bite?"

Allie looked insulted. "Bingo would never bite anyone," she declared. "He's not even wild anymore. Not after a month at John Muir Middle School."

Stephanie raised an eyebrow. "Are you sure?"

Allie frowned. "Stephanie, you've been my best friend practically forever. I wouldn't lie to you."

Stephanie and Allie had met when they sat next to each other on their very first day of kindergarten. They got along right from the start—even though they were complete opposites. Allie was quiet and shy, especially around boys. Stephanie was very outgoing. But Allie and Stephanie also had a lot in common. They both loved reading and music. And animals.

"Hey, what about me?" Darcy demanded.

Darcy was Stephanie's other best friend. She was slim and tall and full of energy. Her family had moved to San Francisco when she was in the sixth grade. For the last four years, Stephanie, Allie, and Darcy were nearly inseparable. They did everything together, and they trusted one another completely.

"I wouldn't lie to either of you," Allie insisted.

"Well, I do trust you, Al," Stephanie replied. "And I totally love Bingo, but I'm not sure if a wild animal is ever completely tame."

"Maybe we should hire a wild-animal trainer to tame him," Darcy said. "That way, no one would have to worry."

Allie gazed at both her friends in disbelief. Then suddenly she shook her head and burst out laughing. "You guys!"

"Gotcha!" Darcy exclaimed.

"You really fell for that one," Stephanie joked. "We know that Bingo doesn't bite. And we know that he loves you."

"Sure he does," Darcy added. "It's like he knows Allie is the one who rescued him when he was hurt."

Stephanie remembered the night Allie found Bingo limping across the school yard. She was coming home after an evening open house, when she and her parents heard a rustling in the grass.

They walked over to investigate, and found

3

the raccoon. His back leg seemed broken. Allie raced inside the school and found Mr. Parasugo, the biology teacher, who luckily had not left yet. He knew all about animals. He also knew whom to call for Bingo—the wildlife advocate center.

The vets from the center examined Bingo. They confirmed that all that was wrong with him was his broken leg. Given the proper care, Bingo's leg would heal, and he could return to normal.

By that time, Allie had grown so attached to Bingo that she convinced Mr. Parasugo to keep him in the biology lab until his foot healed.

"How is Bingo's foot anyway?" Stephanie asked.

"The vet who came in last week said he's better." Allie reported. "He's limping now because of his splint."

Stephanie watched Bingo grab her apple slice with his paws.

He ate the apple, then licked both front paws and the splint on his back foot. The door to the classroom swung open as Mr. Parasugo entered the room. "Hi, girls!" he greeted them. "How's our patient?"

"He's doing great," Allie replied. "Do you know when we can take his splint off?"

Mr. Parasugo pulled out a box full of test tubes from the supply closet. "Probably in one more week," he said. "He's almost all better."

"I'm glad," Allie said. "I love this little guy."

"You're not the only one," Stephanie told her. Tons of kids at John Muir visited Bingo during their free periods. So many kids were playing with him that Mr. Parasugo finally put Allie in charge of raccoon care. It was up to her to make sure he wasn't overfed, and that his cage was cleaned only once a day.

"What happens after his splint comes off?" Stephanie asked.

Mr. Parasugo rubbed his chin. "We'll need to watch him for a little while longer, just to make sure he's okay before we release him."

Josh Linder bounded into the lab and up to Bingo's cage. Josh was the center for John Muir's basketball team, the Raccoons.

"Hey, little guy." Josh poked a finger into the cage and scratched Bingo behind the ear. "How's our favorite team mascot doing?"

"Really well," Mr. Parasugo answered. "I was just telling the girls that we'll be able to release him soon."

"Release him?" Josh was stricken. "No way," he said. "We need Bingo at our big game." He

5

turned to Allie. "It was your idea to make him our mascot, Allie. What do you say?"

"Bingo will definitely be there. He loves going to the basketball games," Allie replied. "As soon as I pick up his cage, he gets all excited. And I know he really brings the team good luck."

"And we need all the luck we can get to win against Kennedy Middle School," Josh added. Kennedy Middle School was John Muir's biggest rival in basketball.

"You know it," Darcy added. "I heard the Kennedy Coyotes really rock this season. We can't let them win!"

Allie stooped down and peered into Bingo's cage. "You're going to help us beat that big, bad Kennedy team, aren't you, Bingo?" she asked. "Yes. I know you think John Muir should win."

Mr. Parasugo smiled. He shook his head in pretend disapproval. "Really, Allie. How can you know what a raccoon is thinking?"

"She knows," Josh replied. "Ever since Allie started bringing Bingo to our games, we've been winning. Bingo broke our three-game losing streak."

Mr. Parasugo laughed. "Couldn't your winning streak have something to do with extra practices and drills?" he asked.

6

Josh shook his head. "I know you're trying to be scientific, Mr. P., but we know better. The day Allie brought this raccoon to school was the day our luck changed. Making him our mascot saved the team."

"I see I won't win this argument." Mr. Parasugo glanced at the clock on the wall. "Well, it's three-thirty," he announced. "I'm staying another fifteen minutes, then I'm leaving for the night. Finish feeding Bingo before then, Allie. Okay?"

"Okay," Allie said.

"So how is the team spirit?" Stephanie asked Josh. "Will we slaughter Kennedy?"

Stephanie met Josh three months earlier when she interviewed him for *The Scribe*, the school newspaper. They'd become really good friends since then.

Josh was in the ninth grade with Stephanie, Darcy, and Allie. He had more school spirit than anyone Stephanie knew. He'd even organized a special pep rally for the day before the big Kennedy game. Every kid at school wanted to win, but no one wanted it more than Josh.

"Trust me—the Raccoons will destroy the Kennedy Coyotes," Josh told Stephanie. "All we have to do is win this game, and then it's on to the semifinals. And then the finals. Nothing can stop us."

"Unless Kennedy pulls another one of their outrageous stunts," Darcy reminded him.

"I still can't believe what they did last year," Stephanie added.

Before last year's big game, Kennedy kids sneaked into the John Muir gym. They painted the hoops and backboards in Kennedy colors. No one could say that was why John Muir lost the game, but it didn't help the team spirit. Stephanie remembered the hours she spent volunteering to repaint the gym.

"Kennedy's the worst," Josh declared. "They deserve to be beaten. They deserve—"

"Ahem!" Mr. Parasugo cleared his throat loudly. "Let's not get carried away, people," he said. "Don't forget—Kennedy's stunt that time was a payback for *our* stunt the game before."

"You mean when John Muir stole the Kennedy cheerleaders' pom-poms?" Stephanie asked, and grinned.

Josh laughed out loud. "That was a dynamite prank."

Mr. Parasugo shook his head wearily. "These rivalries can really get out of hand," he warned.

"But we *have* to win!" Josh frowned. "In the

last five years, Kennedy won ten games and John Muir won nine. We just can't let them take number eleven!"

"Don't worry, Josh," Stephanie told him. She glanced at Bingo. "This time the Raccoons have a secret weapon—a raccoon!"

"Right," Allie agreed. "Bingo won't let us down." She gave Bingo's cage a good-bye pat and picked up her books. "Bye, Mr. P.," she called out to Mr. Parasugo.

Stephanie and Darcy gathered up their books also. They followed Allie and Josh into the hall.

Josh threw them a thumbs-up sign as he hurried toward the gym. "I'd better get to practice," he said. "Don't forget. It's only three weeks till the big game."

"We won't forget," Stephanie told him.

"And neither will Bingo," Allie added. "He'll be there to make sure we win!"

CHAPTER 2

◆ ◀ ◢ ◆

"Let's face it, guys—I'm doomed!" Stephanie brushed a cobweb out of her long blond hair. She waved a hand in disgust at the stacks of dust-covered cartons in the storeroom in her attic.

"I haven't found one interesting thing. And our family-heritage project is due in less than three weeks."

Darcy and Allie lifted a dusty, faded quilt off a trunk. Darcy sneezed. Allie wiped her grimy hands on her jeans.

"Why can't you do your research at the library, like everyone else?" Darcy complained.

"I told you," Stephanie replied. "Libraries are boring! *This* is where my family history is."

"In old cartons and trunks?" Allie asked.

"I'm afraid so," Stephanie answered. "The Tanners never did anything exciting. I asked my dad about them last night. The relatives on my dad's side were mostly teachers and nurses and business owners. We're not in any history books." She began to fold up the dusty quilt.

"You have to write about something," Allie said. "This project counts for *a third* of our history grade this term."

"I know." Stephanie sighed.

"What about your uncle Jesse's side of the family?" Darcy asked. "There must be an interesting story about the Katsopoulis family. I mean, even their name is interesting."

"Not really," Stephanie replied. "I asked Uncle Jesse about them last night at dinner."

"And?" Darcy prodded.

"And he said that in Greece, Katsopoulis is a very ordinary name."

"Well, your dad's side of the family must have done *something*," Darcy suggested.

Stephanie made a face. "Last night my dad said the most interesting members of the Tanner family were probably sitting right at our kitchen table."

"Ugh. You mean he wants you to do research on your sisters?" Allie asked in disbelief.

"Michelle said she'd give me an 'exclusive interview' if I did her chores for a week," Stephanie replied.

Darcy bit back a laugh. "I'm sure interviewing nine-year-old Michelle would be *really* interesting," she said, rolling her eyes.

"About as interesting as interviewing D.J.," Stephanie agreed. D.J. was twenty and in college. "All she talks about is her boring classes. Boring—like my family history. Why couldn't my relatives be like yours?" She turned to Darcy. "I mean, it's so intense that your great-great-great-great-grandmother was a slave. And it is so exciting that your uncle is a scientist for NASA."

"Yeah, Darce. That *is* pretty cool," Allie agreed.

"What about your family?" Darcy asked Allie. "Your grandmother was a flapper back in the twenties. I love that picture of her in that fringed dress."

"And don't forget your cousin," Stephanie added. "The one who helped people escape from Central America in the 1950s? The Taylors did some amazing, exciting, history-making things."

"Come on, Steph—you'll find something to

write about," Allie told her. She pointed to the trunk that had been hidden under the quilt. "Hey—maybe this is where you'll find it," she said.

"*It?*" Stephanie echoed.

"The exciting story you're looking for," Allie explained. "Like, maybe we'll find an old Bible with your whole family tree in it."

"Or a photo album from the turn of the century," Darcy suggested.

"Or a stack of letters," Allie added. "Letters written in this really beautiful old handwriting and scented with perfume," she went on in a dreamy voice.

"That would be pretty romantic," Stephanie agreed. With a burst of excitement, she lifted the lid of the trunk—and pulled out her old Brownie uniform. "Now, this is *incredibly* romantic," she joked.

"What's this thing?" Allie asked. She held up something lumpy and fuzzy.

"It's my first teddy bear," Stephanie told them.

"That's a bear?" Darcy squinted at the ball of fluff.

"Yeah, but I used it so much, you can't recognize it anymore," Stephanie admitted. "Oh, man,

I think my dad saved everything we ever owned."

"No kidding." Darcy pulled out a box marked STEPHANIE'S BABY SHOES and an envelope labeled MICHELLE'S FIRST DRAWINGS.

Allie pulled out a framed photograph and started to laugh.

"What is it?" Stephanie asked.

"A real piece of Tanner history," Allie said.

She handed Stephanie the photograph. Stephanie felt herself blush. It was a picture of herself at age two, on her potty!

"How totally embarrassing!" Stephanie winced. She shoved the photo into the trunk and closed the lid.

Darcy gestured at the stacks of cartons in the storeroom. She shook her head, sending dozens of braids flying against her dark skin. "I hate to say it, Steph, but I don't think you'll find *it* in these cartons. There's so much stuff here, we'll never get through it all."

"Well, these things belong to everyone in the house," Stephanie said. "And this is a pretty full house."

Stephanie's mother had died years earlier in a car accident. Soon after, Stephanie's uncle Jesse moved in to help raise Stephanie and her two sisters. Stephanie's dad, Danny Tanner, couldn't have managed without him. Then Joey Gladstone, who was Danny's good friend, moved in as well.

The house got even more full when Jesse married Becky Donaldson. Becky was Danny Tanner's co-host on the TV show *Wake Up, San Francisco*. Four years after they were married, Jesse and Becky had had twin boys, Nicky and Alex, and they all lived in the attic apartment now. There were nine people—and one dog, Comet, the Tanners' golden retriever—in the house.

The storeroom seemed to contain something from every one of them. Stephanie found her father's bowler hat from his college barbershop quartet, a playpen that the twins had outgrown, a sack of Comet's old chew-toys, and Uncle Jesse's Elvis lamp.

Allie looked at the lamp and wrinkled her nose. "Why would anyone want to keep that scary thing?"

Stephanie grinned. "You know how much Uncle Jesse loves Elvis Presley. The lamp is broken, but I guess he can't bear to throw it out."

Darcy held up a flat basketball. "Okay, maybe

the lamp makes sense. But why would anyone save an old, dead basketball?"

"The Raccoons save their old basketballs," Stephanie said. "It's supposed to be good luck. At least, that's what Josh says."

"I can't believe Josh is so superstitious," Darcy said.

"Yeah. All the guys on the basketball team are really into weird good-luck rituals," Stephanie replied.

"I guess they can't help being a little crazy, with the big game coming up," Darcy said.

"Right." Stephanie opened another carton. "This search is hopeless," she muttered. "A box filled with old books."

Disgusted, she lifted up a tattered copy of *Little Women.* Her eyes narrowed when she saw something sticking out of the pages of the book. She pulled it out.

"Look at this!" Stephanie exclaimed.

"What is it?" Allie asked.

"An old photo from a newspaper," Stephanie said. "There's no date on it, but the paper is really yellow and faded."

"Let's see," Darcy said. She knelt beside Stephanie. "Wow—this woman looks just like you, Steph."

Allie leaned over their shoulders. "Her hair is darker, but otherwise she could *be* you!"

"You're right." Stephanie stared at the photograph in amazement. "This is incredible. It's bizarre!" She read the caption on the photo aloud. *"Jane Tanner, World War Two Spy."*

"Wow! Your relative was a spy?" Darcy asked.

Stephanie glanced at them, her eyes wide with surprise. "I think she's my great-aunt," she said. "My dad's mentioned her once or twice, but no one ever told me she was a spy! I can't believe it."

"This is so cool," Allie said. "You have the most interesting relative of all."

"You're not kidding! A woman spy from World War Two." Darcy's eyes sparkled with excitement. "Wow, Steph. This is big. Very big!"

"You're right." Stephanie grinned. "Well, I guess I don't have to worry about what my heritage project is going to be anymore. Thanks to Great-Aunt Jane, I finally found 'it.' "

CHAPTER
3

◆ ◀ ◆ ◆

"Stephanie! Earth to Stephanie, come in please!"

Stephanie jumped as Darcy grabbed her arm. She nearly tripped as she walked along the sidewalk, away from John Muir Middle School.

"Wh-what?" she asked, totally startled. "Did you say something?"

"Yeah—I said, I thought you wanted to go to the library after school today," Darcy replied.

"I do," Stephanie told her. "I'm supposed to meet Michelle there. Her friend's mom is bringing her over. Then D.J. is coming to do some work and then drive us both home."

"Well, then you must be meeting at some library I've never heard of," Darcy said. "Be-

18

cause *our* public library is in the opposite direction."

Stephanie glanced at the surrounding streets. Darcy was absolutely right. "Oops," she said, feeling embarrassed. She turned back toward the library.

Darcy walked along beside her.

"Isn't Allie coming?" Stephanie asked.

"She couldn't," Darcy said. "She just found out that the vet is going to remove Bingo's splint today. Allie didn't want to miss that."

"No, she wouldn't," Stephanie replied. "I'm so glad Bingo is all better."

"So is everyone," Darcy agreed. She paused, then shot Stephanie a concerned look. "But what's up with you?" she asked. "Your body was at school today, but your mind sure wasn't. All day long you've been walking around in a daze."

"It's this spy business," Stephanie confessed. "Ever since I found that photograph yesterday, I've been thinking about my great-aunt Jane. I guess I was daydreaming a little."

"A little?" Darcy asked.

"I can't help wondering what her life must have been like," Stephanie explained. "I mean, every day I go to school and then I go home and have dinner with my family. At night I do my homework. Sometimes I hang out with you and Allie. Or if things get *really* exciting, I go to a school basketball game."

"Steph, that's what most middle school kids do," Darcy pointed out as they approached the library. "We go to school. We hang out with our friends and our families."

"Well, you've got to admit, it's boring compared to the life my great-aunt led," Stephanie said.

She pictured her aunt dressed as she had been in the newspaper photo—in a trench coat with a fedora angled across her forehead.

"All those secrets," Stephanie murmured. "Nights filled with cloak-and-dagger excitement. Just imagine the amazing adventures she must have had in foggy London. I bet that she—"

"Stephanie!" Michelle interrupted. She waited at the top of the library stairs with her hands on her hips. "D.J. is already here. She just went inside to look for you," she called. "Hurry up."

Stephanie groaned. "And *my* excitement is being bossed around by a nine-year-old."

"What makes you think your great-aunt the

spy didn't have to deal with her family?" Darcy asked as they reached Michelle at the top of the steps.

"What great-aunt?" Michelle demanded.

Darcy gazed at Michelle in surprise. "Didn't Stephanie tell you that your great-aunt Jane was a spy?"

"No way," Michelle said. "Last night Dad said she was a schoolteacher."

"Oh, Michelle. You're easily fooled!" Stephanie told her. "That was probably just her cover." She opened her notebook and showed Michelle the yellowed newspaper photograph.

Michelle's blue eyes widened. "She *was* a spy! This is amazing."

"I know," Stephanie said. "One of our relatives actually risked her life for her country."

"Come on," Darcy said. She opened the library door. "Let's see if we can find out more about her."

An hour later the table Stephanie was sharing with Darcy and Michelle was covered with books. There were books on World War II and books on famous spies.

"Look at this article." Stephanie folded back

the pages of a slim magazine. "It's called 'Tips for Future Spies,' " she whispered.

"Sounds great," Darcy whispered back. "Did you find anything about Jane Tanner yet?"

"Nope," Stephanie replied. "Just a lot of stories about Mata Hari."

"What's a Mata Hari?" Michelle asked. "It sounds like some kind of car."

"It's a person," Stephanie explained. "Mata Hari was a name she made up. She was a famous spy—a Dutch double agent." She showed Michelle a photograph of a small, dark-haired woman.

"What's a double agent?" Michelle asked.

"That means she worked for two countries," Stephanie said. "She spied for both the French and the Germans during the First World War. She was supposed to be very exotic."

"Cool!" Michelle said.

"I think I've heard of her," Darcy remarked. "But didn't her story have a really gross ending?"

"It was pretty grim," Stephanie agreed.

Michelle seemed fascinated. "What do you mean?" she asked. "Tell me."

"Well, the French caught on to her," Stephanie said. "They executed her by firing squad."

22

Michelle looked alarmed. "Maybe that's why Great-Aunt Jane got out of the spy business and became a teacher."

"Girls!" Ms. Craven, the librarian, glared at them. "Please keep you voices down!"

"Sorry," Stephanie murmured.

Darcy reached for the magazine. She flipped through the pages of "Tips for Future Spies" and read the headings aloud. " 'Obtaining False Identification,' 'Lock Picking Made Easy,' 'Living with a Secret Identity,' 'Breaking Codes and Recognizing Secret Signals,' 'Handy Phrases for Crossing International Borders . . .' "

She put the magazine down. "This won't have any information on your great-aunt Jane," she said.

"Maybe not," Stephanie replied. "But I'm not sure that the specifics really matter."

"What does that mean?" Darcy asked.

"Well, I already feel as though I know Jane Tanner. I mean, I can see her so clearly . . ."

Stephanie closed her eyes. She imagined Jane in a ballroom beneath a great crystal chandelier. The black-and-white marble floor gleamed in the light. Everywhere she looked she saw beautiful women in gorgeous evening gowns and handsome, dashing men in tuxedos.

An orchestra played dreamy music. Waiters moved noiselessly around the room, carrying silver trays filled with tiny sandwiches.

Jane Tanner entered. Her dark hair gleamed on her shoulders. Diamonds sparkled at her ears and throat. A white feather boa was draped over her elegant golden gown.

An incredibly handsome man approached her. "Mademoiselle Tanner?" he murmured.

"Perhaps," she replied.

"May I have this dance?"

Jane hesitated—until she spotted the pale yellow carnation pinned to his jacket.

"The signal," she murmured. "You are one of us. My contact."

The gentleman bowed. "But of course," he answered.

Jane held out her hand. A sapphire glittered on her ring finger. A diamond bracelet sparkled on her wrist.

The handsome man pulled her into his arms. Together they whirled around the ballroom. Jane's golden skirt skimmed the floor.

The man began to speak in a low voice. "You will go to Paris tomorrow," he informed her. "There you will pose as Countess d'Arcy. You must look for Count Christophe. He will give you the papers that you must take to Germany."

"I understand," Jane murmured.

"Do you?" the man replied. "Can you possibly understand how dangerous this mission really is?"

"Of course," Jane told him. "There was never any question. I would do anything for my country. . . ."

"Stephanie!" Darcy's voice snapped her back to reality. "You're doing it again," Darcy warned.

Stephanie flushed. "Sorry," she murmured. She glanced up and spotted D.J. walking toward them. D.J. was totally focused on the book she held open in her hand. Michelle slipped out of her chair and sneaked up behind D.J. D.J. stopped suddenly and Michelle crashed into her.

D.J. jumped in surprise. "Michelle!" She frowned at her youngest sister. "What on earth are you doing?"

"I was trying to sneak up on you, like a spy. Like Great-Aunt Jane," Michelle said.

D.J. frowned. "What are you talking about? She was a schoolteacher, not a lunatic."

"She was a spy," Michelle informed her. "Stephanie found an old newspaper photograph that proves it."

D.J. looked questioningly at Stephanie. Stephanie showed her the clipping.

"I don't know," D.J. remarked. "Dad never said anything about us having spies in the family."

"Maybe Aunt Jane never told anyone in the family," Stephanie said. "Maybe she was never allowed to tell anyone in her whole life."

"Maybe," D.J. said, but she sounded doubtful.

Stephanie gave a wistful sigh. "I bet she met all sorts of famous people," she said.

"And she probably knew all sorts of neat secret codes and signals," Michelle added.

D.J. nodded toward the far side of the room. "Like those signals?" she asked.

Stephanie saw Josh Linder and three other guys on the John Muir basketball team. They were going through one of their good-luck rituals. They slapped both palms together, spun around, and slapped again behind their backs.

Then they touched right elbows and jabbed their left shoulders. Then they all recited, "High-five, take a dive, meet me around the other side."

"What *are* they doing?" Darcy stared at them openmouthed.

Stephanie groaned. "Josh told me about this.

Whenever guys on the team meet, they have to do that greeting. It's for good luck."

"Quiet!" Ms. Craven told the boys.

"Oh, no," Stephanie said. "Ms. Craven interrupted. Now they have to start all over again!"

D.J. laughed as the boys repeated the ritual. This time they whispered the words.

Stephanie muffled a laugh.

"If real spies used signals like those, we'd probably have lost the war." D.J. turned to the girls. "Listen, I've got to look up one more thing in the reference room. I'll be back in ten minutes. Steph, would you watch Michelle?"

"Sure," Stephanie said.

"Hey, Steph," Josh greeted her as he hurried up to her table. "Were you laughing at us?" he asked, pretending to be hurt.

"It was kind of hard not to," Stephanie answered.

"I know. Those rituals do look kind of silly," he admitted. "But they keep the team together."

"They ought to keep you apart," Darcy joked. "I heard that none of you has changed your socks since your last game."

"Is that true?" Stephanie asked.

Josh grinned. "It's for good luck," he explained. "We were wearing those socks when we won the game."

"Yuck!" Michelle said.

Josh laughed. "I'd better go," he said. "Ms. Craven's giving us her evil eye. But I'll call you later, Steph. I want to ask your opinion on my English essay. You're a good writer. I could use some tips."

"No problem. Later," Stephanie said.

Darcy made a face. "Yuck is right," she told Stephanie. "I wouldn't go near any of those guys until basketball season is over."

"Definitely not," Stephanie said. "I think we should—"

She broke off as Allie rushed through the library doors. Allie paused for a moment near the front desk. Her chest was heaving and she was gasping for breath. She looked as though she'd run all the way from school.

Allie's eyes scanned the reading room frantically.

"Uh-oh," Stephanie said. "What's going on?"

Stephanie and Darcy leaped up and hurried across the room.

"Allie, what's wrong?" Stephanie asked as they neared the front desk.

"Shhh!" Ms. Craven called.

"Something terrible has happened!" Allie exclaimed. Tears began to stream down her face. "I—I went to the bio lab to watch the vet take off Bingo's splint. . . ." She stopped.

"And?" Stephanie prompted.

Allie wrung her hands. "And—his cage door was open. Oh, Stephanie, Bingo is gone!"

CHAPTER
4

♦ ◂ ◆ ♦

"Any more news about Bingo?" Stephanie asked as she rushed up to Darcy and Allie. They were waiting for her at their usual before-school meeting place—the pay phone near the gym.

Allie's eyes were red and puffy. "No news," she said in a small voice. "He's still missing."

"I was telling her not to worry," Darcy said. "We'll find him today, I'm sure."

"Oh, Steph, what if Bingo ran out of school?" Allie swallowed hard. "What if he's lost in the middle of San Francisco? This is a big, busy city. He could run out in the middle of traffic, or—"

Stephanie put an arm around her friend. "Listen," she said. "Bingo's smart. He's going to be okay. And we're going to find him.'

Allie's voice quivered. "Wh-what if we don't?"

"We will," Darcy promised.

"We have to," Josh said, coming up to them. "The basketball team needs that little guy. We can't play Kennedy without him."

Darcy glared at him. "How can you think about the basketball game now? Bingo was special to Allie. He was like—well—like her pet. She's not allowed to have pets at home."

"Gee, I didn't know. I'm sorry," Josh muttered.

"That's okay," Allie told him. "It's just that Bingo is out there, totally lost, and I'm so worried. He didn't even get his dinner last night."

"Hey, we'll find him," Josh told her. "Definitely. After all, the whole school needs Bingo. He's the best thing that's happened at John Muir in a long time. Uh—and I don't just mean as the basketball mascot," he added as Darcy shot him a warning look.

"How do you think he got out anyway?" Josh went on. "Was something wrong with the door on his cage? Could he have gotten out by himself?"

Stephanie listened as Allie answered the same

questions that she and Darcy had asked the previous afternoon.

"The cage is fine," Allie reported in a flat voice. "That was the first thing we checked. There was no way he could open it himself, the vet said."

"I see." Josh tapped Stephanie's shoulder. "Can I talk to you a minute, Steph?" he asked in a low voice.

He and Stephanie stepped away from Allie and Darcy.

"What's up?" Stephanie asked him.

Josh hesitated. "Listen, don't tell Allie yet," he said. "But the basketball team has a theory about how Bingo got out."

Now what? Stephanie wondered. *They probably think Bingo ran away because they changed their underwear or something.*

Josh took a deep breath. "We think Bingo was kidnapped."

"Kidnapped?" Stephanie stared at Josh in confusion. "Who would kidnap a hurt raccoon?"

"The Kennedy Coyotes," Josh replied.

"Kennedy's basketball team?" Stephanie shook her head. "That's crazy."

"Think about it. It makes perfect sense," Josh insisted. "They've pulled some pretty wild stunts before. And everyone there knows Bingo brings us luck. They know we haven't lost a game since we got him."

"Wow," Stephanie murmured. "You may have a point."

"Bingo is our secret weapon," Josh went on. "And now Kennedy has him!"

"But that's just a guess," Stephanie pointed out. "We don't know that Bingo didn't get out by accident. I mean, a John Muir kid might have forgotten to close his cage door."

"Maybe," Josh said. "But I came in early and talked to my coach about this whole thing. Then we went and talked to Mr. Parasugo. They agree with me. They think someone let Bingo out on purpose."

Stephanie felt shocked. "Then, it really could be true?"

"Yup," Josh replied. "Mr. P. just called the police to report it."

"What did the police say?" Stephanie asked.

Josh shrugged. "They said they're sorry, but they have more important things to do than figure out how a raccoon got out of his cage."

"So they're not going to help us find him?" Stephanie said.

"Nope," Josh told her. "We'll lose the game if we don't find Bingo in time."

"This is a disaster," Stephanie murmured.

Josh kicked one foot against a nearby locker. "I wish I could be a fly on the wall in the Kennedy locker room," he said. "I wish we could find Bingo. If we could only spy on those raccoon-stealing skunks!"

Spy on them? Stephanie thought. *I wonder . . .*

Josh was still talking, but Stephanie wasn't listening. She was too busy arguing with herself.

Don't even think about it. It's outrageous, she told herself.

Well, maybe you could try—if you didn't take it too seriously, she rationalized.

But what would I do anyway? she wondered.

Who knows? Think of what Great-Aunt Jane would do, she thought.

"But I really think this should be our secret," Josh continued.

"Huh?" Stephanie blinked. "Sorry, Josh, I wasn't listening. What did you say?"

"I said, I don't think we should tell Allie about the kidnapping idea," Josh replied.

"You're probably right," Stephanie agreed. "She's already so upset about Bingo being missing. She'd feel even worse if she thought he was stolen."

"Yeah. Who knows what those Kennedy kids might do to him?" Josh's expression was grim.

"Yikes. Let's agree not to tell Allie about it," Stephanie said.

"Steph!" Darcy and Allie hurried over to Stephanie and Josh. "Guess what? Allie and I had the best idea. We're going to organize a schoolwide search for Bingo. We'll start this afternoon right after school. We'll check all the storage rooms and closets. We'll make sure he's not hiding in anyone's locker. Then we'll go over the grounds outside."

"Oh," Stephanie said. "That's a really good idea!" *Except that Bingo probably isn't anywhere around here.*

"So, can you be in our search party?" Allie asked.

"Actually, I can't," Stephanie said. "I have a dentist appointment this afternoon, remember?"

"Oh, right." Allie looked disappointed. "I guess you can't reschedule it for another day, can you?"

"Are you kidding?" Stephanie replied. "My dad would kill me. I'm really sorry, you guys."

"That's okay. We understand," Allie told her.

"We'll call you tonight and tell you what happened."

Darcy sighed. "I sure hope we find Bingo. I hate to think of him lost in the city."

I hate to think of him kidnapped, Stephanie added to herself.

"Oh, I'm sure we'll find him," Allie said, forcing a cheerful grin. "All we need is a little good luck."

"No, what we need is a good search team," Darcy corrected Allie.

You're both wrong, Stephanie thought to herself. *What we need is a really good spy. And maybe that spy is me!*

CHAPTER
5

◆ ◂ ▸ ◆

Stephanie hurried to the bus stop after her dentist appointment. She couldn't wait to get home to call Allie and Darcy. She had to know what happened with their search.

Maybe Bingo is already back at school, she thought.

The bus stop was on a busy corner in Noe Valley. Noe Valley was an older neighborhood with steep, narrow streets and rows of attached wooden houses. The bus stop was in the shopping area. Boutiques, coffee houses, and gift shops lined the sidewalks.

Stephanie examined the shops as she waited. She spotted a brightly striped awning nearby.

Cheerful green letters announced that it was Valdi's Pizza. She glanced at the window—and gasped. A large orange banner hung in the window. KENNEDY HIGH was spelled across it in shining silver letters.

Of course. Stephanie felt a burst of excitement. Noe Valley was near Kennedy Middle School.

She took a step closer and peered in through the window. Valdi's looked like a typical pizza parlor. In fact, it looked a lot like Tony's, the pizzeria where the John Muir kids hung out.

Should I go in? she asked herself. *Would Great-Aunt Jane go in?* She paused to consider. *Definitely!*

She stepped inside the narrow restaurant, trying not to grin. She was in "enemy territory."

My first spy mission! she thought. *Cool!*

The smells of garlic and tomato sauce filled the air. The booths were covered in red upholstery, and the tables and walls were white. There were no video games as there were in Tony's. An old-fashioned jukebox played one of her favorite songs. Stephanie glanced around. The place was filled with kids her age.

What would Great-Aunt Jane do now? she asked herself.

She stared at the menu posted on the counter,

trying to picture her glamorous great-aunt in the middle of a pizza parlor.

"Which do you like?" asked a friendly voice in line behind her. "Thin crust or thick?"

Stephanie turned. A girl with wavy red hair and brown eyes stood behind her. "Uh, thick crust, I guess," Stephanie said.

"I can't decide." The girl gave her a thoughtful look. "I don't think I've seen you around before."

"Um, no, you haven't," Stephanie blurted out.

"Did you just start at Kennedy?" the girl asked.

"I—uh . . . yeah, I did."

"Well, I'm Laura Walker," the girl said. She smiled at Stephanie, expecting her to introduce herself.

Stephanie smiled to cover her panic. Her mind was racing. She couldn't tell Laura her real name, could she? Spies never gave away their identity.

"I'm, uh, Jane. . . ." Stephanie glanced at the menu again: The third item listed was a cheese calzone.

"Calzo!" she finished. "Jane Calzo."

"This is Sherri Ruiz." Laura pointed to the dark-haired girl standing beside her.

"Hey, where are you sitting?" Sherri asked.

Stephanie shrugged. "I don't know," she answered.

"Why don't you sit with us?" Laura said.

"That'd be great," Stephanie said. "Thanks."

They finally ordered and their slices were ready in a minute.

"We've got the booth by the window," Laura told Stephanie. "Follow me."

Wow! Stephanie thought. *This is amazing. I already met two kids from Kennedy—and they're totally buying my story. This spy thing is easy. I'll track down Bingo in no time.*

Stephanie carried her tray to the booth. Sherri and Laura sat down beside her. Sherri dug into her pepperoni slice. Laura sipped a tall chocolate shake.

"So, I guess you just moved here?" Sherri asked.

"Yeah," Stephanie said. She felt a pang of guilt. It was a total lie. But then, spies had to make up cover stories. That was different from lying.

"Actually, today was my first day," Stephanie added.

Laura gave her a sympathetic look. "What a

time to start," she said. "Kennedy's going a little crazy right now."

"What do you mean?" Stephanie asked.

"All the pep rallies and posters and stuff. They're all over the school. There's a big game coming up," Sherri explained. "Our basketball team, the Coyotes, is going to play John Muir Middle School's Raccoons. They're our major rivals." She shook her head. "Our team is out for blood."

"They always are when we play Muir." Laura glanced at Stephanie's untouched pizza. "Aren't you hungry?"

"Oh, yeah, of course," Stephanie said. She was so wrapped up in being an undercover spy, she'd totally forgotten to eat. She took a bite of pizza. "What's the deal with Kennedy and Muir?" she asked.

Laura shrugged. "Beats me. It's a really old rivalry. I mean, none of us even knows the kids at John Muir."

"Right," Sherri agreed. "I guess it's kind of dumb that everyone makes it sound like they're the enemy or something."

Stephanie stared at them both. It was the last thing she'd expected to hear from a Kennedy kid. She always thought they were bad news.

"So, is Kennedy really serious about basketball?" she asked, to cover her surprise.

"Totally rabid!" Laura replied. "I mean, we've got a good team. We all want to see them win."

"They have to win," Sherri added. "It's some kind of honor thing."

It sounds like they're really psyched. But enough to kidnap Bingo? Stephanie wondered.

"What grade are you in?" Sherri asked.

"Ninth," Stephanie answered.

"So are we," Laura said. "Who've you got for English?"

Stephanie froze. She couldn't make up a name. They'd know she was lying. "Uh . . ." She felt herself blushing. "I can't remember," she finally said. "I—I had so many new teachers today, I can't keep any of them straight."

Laura laughed. "I know what you mean. I felt the same way on my first day at Kennedy. It's so confusing, trying to find your way around *and* remember who everyone is."

"Right." Stephanie felt a wave of relief. But if the conversation went on much longer, she'd have a hard time keeping up her cover. She needed time to figure out answers to all the usual questions: Where do you live? Where did you move from? Who's your homeroom teacher?

She glanced at her watch. "Oh, no," she moaned. "I totally forgot, I told my dad I'd be home by five." She shot Laura and Sherri an apologetic look. "I'm sorry, but I have to go."

She stood up. "Hope I see you around," she said.

"What about tomorrow?" Sherri said.

"Tomorrow?" Stephanie echoed.

"Yeah, tomorrow's Saturday," Sherri answered. "A bunch of kids from Kennedy go to that bowling alley, The Super Bowl, every Saturday. Why don't you come along? If you like bowling, that is."

"Come along . . . uh . . ." Stephanie paused, startled by the invitation. She hadn't really thought about seeing them again.

But it's your lucky break, she thought. *You can ask all sorts of questions. You can learn the truth about Bingo. Great-Aunt Jane would definitely go for it.*

"Sure. Great," Stephanie said. "I like bowling." She smiled at her new "friends."

"Okay. Meet you there around two," Laura told her. "See you then."

"Yeah, see you," Stephanie responded.

She flew out of Valdi's, amazed at her own luck. It had to be fate that she met Laura and

Sherri. But they believed her cover story. They believed she was Jane Calzo, Kennedy student! They invited her to go bowling with them the next day.

I can do this, Stephanie thought. She nearly skipped to the bus stop. *I have Great-Aunt Jane's talent!*

And I can be John Muir Middle School's hero. I, Stephanie Tanner, can single-handedly find Bingo and bring him home!

CHAPTER
6

◆ ◄ ▸ ◆

Stephanie glanced at her bedside clock. One o'clock already! She had exactly forty minutes before she had to leave for The Super Bowl.

She crossed her legs and leaned over the map of San Francisco that was spread across her bed. Luckily, Michelle was out shopping with D.J. and Becky. Stephanie was glad to have the room to herself. She needed to concentrate on her second spy mission.

She studied the map. Jane Calzo lived on Covington Street, she decided. It was a small street at the edge of the Kennedy school district.

The doorbell rang downstairs. "Steph-a-neeeee!" Nicky shouted. "It's for you."

Great! They're here. Stephanie bounded down the stairs. Allie and Darcy stood in the entryway, talking to her uncle Jesse. Jesse tried to hold a squirming Nicky by the hand.

"And that was the last time anyone saw Bingo," Allie was saying.

"You had no luck searching around the school?" Jesse asked.

"None," Allie said. She forced a brave smile. "But we're not giving up. We're going to find him."

"Darce, Allie," Stephanie called. "Come on upstairs!"

Allie and Darcy followed Stephanie up to her room.

"So, what's the big secret you had to tell us— in private?" Darcy demanded as soon as the door was closed. She pushed aside the mound of stuffed animals on Michelle's bed and sat down.

Allie eyed the map and books on Stephanie's bed. "What are you doing?" she asked. "Working on your heritage project?"

"Sort of," Stephanie said. "Mostly, I'm getting ready for my second spy mission."

"Spy mission? What are you talking about?" Allie asked.

Stephanie decided she had to tell Allie that

Bingo might have been kidnapped. After she calmed Allie down, she told both Darcy and Allie what had happened the day before at Valdi's.

"So let me get this straight," Darcy said. "You actually spied on a bunch of kids from Kennedy?"

"Yeah." Stephanie grinned. "I felt like I had invaded enemy territory. It was really kind of exciting."

"Wow. You were brave to go over there." Darcy gazed at her in admiration.

"I can't believe you did it," Allie agreed. "And now you're about to go bowling with them?"

"Right," Stephanie said. "And I need you two to help."

"This is incredible," Darcy declared. "Steph, you're not only brave. You're an absolute genius!"

Allie's eyes shone with excitement. "It's so wonderful that you're doing this for Bingo."

"For Bingo and you, and Josh, and all of John Muir Middle School," Stephanie added.

"Well, we're all really lucky," Darcy said. "What a break that your dentist is in Kennedy territory."

"I know," Stephanie replied. "But I'm a little

worried. If the Kennedy kids ask me more questions, I'm afraid they'll figure out I'm a fake."

"What kind of questions?" Allie asked.

"Like where did I move from?" Stephanie replied. "And who do I have for English?"

"The first one's easy," Darcy said. "You have to say you came from a place that's far away, so there's less chance of someone catching you. I mean, you can't say you just moved here from Palo Alto. Someone at Kennedy might know kids in Palo Alto."

"She's right," Allie said. "Why don't you tell them you moved from . . . upstate New York? I have cousins there. They go to Oneonta Middle School. I think their team is called the Owls. I've seen pictures of their school. It's a modern building—all glass walls and ramps connecting the different levels."

"That's great," Stephanie said. She wrote the information in her notebook. It was now her spy journal. "My book of spy tips says it's vital to have convincing details when you go undercover."

Allie reached into her pack and pulled out the local paper.

"What are you doing?" Stephanie asked.

"Trying to find the name of a Kennedy English

teacher," Allie replied. "I saw an article this morning about Kennedy sponsoring an essay contest. Here it is. 'Ms. Frances Dolan, who teaches eighth- and ninth-grade English, will be judging the contest . . .'" Allie read aloud.

"Perfect!" Stephanie said. She wrote down *Ms. Dolan* in her notebook. "I just hope I can remember all this. Now I hope I don't run into any John Muir kids at The Super Bowl."

"Not very likely," Darcy told her. "They don't hang out in Noe Valley. Or go bowling there."

"Right." Stephanie closed her notebook. She glanced up at her friends. "Thanks, guys. I needed help, and you really came through."

"Well, Bingo needs us all," Allie said.

"And so does the John Muir team," Darcy said. "The big game is exactly two weeks away!"

"No problem," Stephanie told her. "How long can it take to find one little raccoon? Maybe I can even have Bingo back by the end of the day!"

CHAPTER
7

◆ ◀ ◆ ◆

But Stephanie didn't feel so confident as she pulled open the door of The Super Bowl. She took a deep breath. Her stomach was doing somersaults. The echo of bowling balls spinning down the lanes mixed with the crash of pins hitting the smooth wood floors. She walked quickly into the coat room and hung up her jacket. Then she headed for the rental desk.

She changed her shoes, glancing around but trying not to be obvious. The bowling lanes were crowded. She didn't see Sherri or Laura anywhere. What if they didn't show up?

Calm down, she told herself. *Imagine you're Great-Aunt Jane.* Stephanie pictured Jane in bowling shoes, pants, and a loose shirt with her name and two little bowling pins embroidered on the pocket. *Jane Tanner would fit right in*, Stephanie realized. *She'd act like bowling with kids from Kennedy was the most natural thing in the world.*

"Jane! Jane!" A girl with short black hair and very blue eyes rushed up to her. "Hi," she said. "Are you Jane Calzo?"

Stephanie bit her tongue to keep from saying, No, my name is Stephanie. She smiled. "Yeah. How'd you know?" she asked.

"I'm a friend of Laura's," the girl explained. "My name is Dana Pugnosian." She rolled her eyes. "I know, pug nose. Pugnosian—with a name like that, I get a lot of jokes."

Stephanie grinned. Dana was funny—and very pretty.

"Laura called me and said you'd be here," Dana went on. "She can't come today. She got stuck baby-sitting her little brother."

"Oh. I know what that's like," Stephanie murmured.

"Yeah, and Sherri got drafted for a family shopping trip," Dana went on. "So Laura asked me to come and meet you."

"That was really nice of her," Stephanie said.

"She knew I was just the one to help you,"

Dana said. "I moved here last year. I've been the new kid at school. But don't worry. Kennedy kids are pretty decent. You won't have trouble making friends."

"Actually, everyone's been really nice so far," Stephanie admitted. *I wonder when I'll meet the really horrible kids from Kennedy*, she added to herself.

"Why don't you bowl on my team," Dana said. "We're bowling against the guys and we're one person short."

"Sure," Stephanie said. "Thanks."

Dana led her to a lane at the other end of the bowling alley. She introduced the girls first. "Jane Calzo, meet Alexis, Zoe, and Maria."

Stephanie nodded at the other girls. Alexis and Zoe both had long brown hair. Maria had short-cropped, curly black hair and the most intense blue eyes Stephanie had ever seen.

Dana gestured to five tall, lanky boys who were horsing around on the other side of the lane. "That's Scott, Charlie, Paul, Malcolm, and Billy," she said.

"They're all so tall," Stephanie remarked.

Dana grinned. "That's because they're all Coyotes. They're on Kennedy's basketball team," she added.

"Really?" Stephanie tried hard to look casual. *This is fantastic. I must have been meant to be a spy.*

She couldn't believe her luck. She was about to spend the afternoon with the Kennedy basketball team—her prime suspects! It was too perfect.

"Don't worry," Dana said, misunderstanding Stephanie's expression. "They don't bowl nearly as well as they play basketball."

Dana picked up one of the score sheets. "We already beat them in the first game."

"And we had one less player," Alexis added.

"That was just luck," Malcolm scoffed.

"You wish," Zoe shot back.

"You jocks are all so smug," Maria teased. "You just wait. You'll be lucky if you win a frame all afternoon." She grinned at Stephanie. "Especially now that we've evened out the numbers."

"Yeah, yeah," Billy said with a grin. "Just bowl and we'll see."

Stephanie sat down on the girls' side of the lane. It suddenly occurred to her that she wasn't much of a bowler. What if the girls were really competitive—and she made them lose?

She tried not to groan out loud. *I bet Great-Aunt Jane was a terrific bowler,* she thought.

Dana bowled first. She knocked down eight

pins. Then Billy got a spare. Zoe went next and also scored eight. Malcolm got a strike. The guys all slapped high-fives and cheered. They were winning.

Stephanie was up next. She scooped up the ball and approached the lane. Then she stepped forward and sent the heavy ball spinning— straight into the gutter!

"Oh, no," she exclaimed.

"It's probably just nerves," Dana told her. "You'll do better on your next try."

"I hope," Stephanie muttered.

"Come on, Jane, you can do it!" Zoe cheered as Stephanie waited for the ball to return.

Stephanie felt everyone watching her. She was about to bowl another gutter ball. She knew it!

"Wait, Jane," Dana hurried up to her. "Just relax," she suggested. "Keep your eyes on the center of the lane. And let your weight fall forward as you release the ball."

"Okay," Stephanie said. She took a few deep breaths and shook out her arms, trying to relax. Then she kept her eyes on the center of the lane and tried to fall forward as Dana said.

She released the ball. It whirled down the center of the lane. At the last moment it zigged to the right. But it knocked down four pins.

"Way to go!" Maria shouted.

Dana flashed her a thumbs-up sign. "You're doing great."

Stephanie felt a burst of pride. *I was better—and they're cheering me on. Even though I'm a terrible bowler!* She frowned. *But, that's so—so—nice. . . .*

Stephanie sat down as a boy took his turn. Her head was spinning in confusion. Was she actually starting to like the kids from Kennedy? They were the enemy, weren't they?

Her thoughts were interrupted when she realized one of the boys was sitting down next to her.

"I'm Billy," he said.

"I remember," Stephanie said.

"So, how do you like Kennedy so far?" Billy asked. He flushed lightly under his freckles and ran a hand through his short brown hair. The light glinted off his wire-rimmed glasses. He wasn't super good-looking, Stephanie thought. But there was something attractive about him.

"Kennedy is really different from my other school," Stephanie stated cautiously. "I mean, San Francisco and Oneonta are nothing alike."

"I believe that," Billy said. "So . . . do you like basketball?"

"Sure—when the teams are good," Stephanie replied.

"Well, Kennedy is the best in the city," Billy boasted. "No question."

Stephanie stiffened. *No way! John Muir has the best team in the city,* she thought. But she forced herself not to react.

"So, what's the story on John Muir?" Stephanie asked.

"They're the enemy. Our major rival," Billy explained. "And they've got a real strong team this year. But we're going to beat them, for sure. All we need is no injuries—and a little luck."

"Luck?" Stephanie repeated. "What does a basketball team like Kennedy's do for good luck?"

"You wouldn't believe it if I told you." Billy looked embarrassed.

"I might," Stephanie replied. "Back in Oneonta, our team used to do crazy stuff. Like, if they won, they wouldn't wash their hair between games."

Billy wrinkled his nose. "Yuck! We're not *that* gross! But, hey, I say, do whatever works." He gave a good-natured shrug.

"You know what really worked in Oneonta?" Stephanie went on. "Our *mascot.* Our team was called the Oneonta Owls, and someone started bringing an owl to the games. And—"

"Hey, that's just like the Raccoons," Billy broke in. "Some girl at John Muir found this injured raccoon, and now they bring it to all their games. They haven't lost since then."

"Really? Sounds like Kennedy better get Muir's mascot away from them," Stephanie suggested in a teasing voice.

She stole a glance at Billy. She could feel the pulse in her throat jumping. This was it! This was the moment when Billy would tell her that they already *did* get him, that they had Bingo!

Billy just shrugged again. "Our coach says all we need is practice and determination. He's not real big on superstitions or mascots."

"Oh," Stephanie said. She felt a wave of disappointment.

"Yo, Billy, stop flirting with the enemy," Malcolm called. "You're up!"

Enemy? Stephanie stiffened. How did Malcolm know she was from John Muir? How did he know that she was a spy?

She glanced at Malcolm and she realized he was just teasing—he was talking about her being on the girls' bowling team.

Billy touched her wrist lightly. "Catch you

later, Jane. Okay?" He gave her a lopsided grin and hurried back to his lane.

Then Malcolm's other comment sunk in.

Wait a minute! Was Billy really flirting with me? Stephanie wondered. He was paying a lot of attention, and really watching me. She felt her heart give a strange little lurch. *He really* was *kind of cute,* she caught herself thinking.

Stop it, she told herself. *You're just imagining things.*

Dana plopped down beside her. "So—" she said in a teasing voice. "I think Billy Dean likes you!"

Stephanie felt herself starting to blush.

"The question is, do you like Billy?" Dana asked.

"I—I don't know," Stephanie answered. "I just met him."

Dana nodded. "That's true. But just so you know, Billy's a really great guy."

"He seems nice," Stephanie answered. She felt a prick of discomfort. Billy *was* really nice. So far, everyone she had met from Kennedy was nice. For an instant she found herself wondering why everyone at John Muir hated them so much.

"Hey, I've got an idea!" Dana burst out.

"What?" Stephanie asked.

"Well, there's only one way you'll know if you could like Billy—you need another chance to talk with him, right?" Dana waited eagerly for Stephanie's reply.

"Right . . ." Stephanie nodded. She wasn't sure what Dana was getting at.

"Great. Wednesday night, we're all going to decorate the team bus," Dana told her. "We're meeting in the parking lot behind Kennedy at seven. The whole team will be there—including Billy. It will be tons of fun. So why don't you come, too? That way you and Billy can get to know each other better."

"Um, well . . ." Stephanie felt torn. On one hand, it was exactly what she needed. She had to stick close to the Kennedy kids to find more clues about Bingo.

On the other hand, she was starting to feel a little guilty. She kind of liked Dana and her friends. Could she keep pretending to be Jane Calzo? She felt as if she were playing a dirty trick on them.

Then she remembered Allie's face when she found out Bingo was missing.

And she remembered Josh. The team had worked so hard to get back its winning pace.

Without Bingo, all that hard work would go right down the drain, he believed.

And what about all the other kids at John Muir?

Am I nuts? Stephanie asked herself. *I can't let any of them down.*

Finding Bingo was all that really mattered.

Stephanie Tanner—also known as Jane Calzo, superspy—had the Kennedy kids completely snowed. She *had* to keep spying. She was the only one who could do it.

"Decorating the bus sounds like fun," she told Dana. "I'll definitely be there."

"I'm glad. Now let's finish our game," Dana said.

Stephanie cheered as loudly as anyone when they beat the boys' team. She chatted and laughed with Maria and Alexis as they returned their bowling shoes and headed for the coat room. The rest of the Kennedy crew followed close behind.

"Now, where did I put my jacket?" Stephanie muttered as she shoved coats aside.

Then she saw it. Hidden behind a row of hanging coats.

A wire cage.

Inside the cage she caught sight of a tuft of fur. Gray fur. Exactly like Bingo's!

CHAPTER
8

◆ ◀ ◢ ◆

Dana reached out toward the gray fur.

"I knew it! I knew you had him!" Stephanie exclaimed. She turned accusingly to Dana.

"Jane, what are you talking about?" Dana looked bewildered.

"This!" Stephanie pointed to the cage. "What do you think you're doing with *this?*"

Dana glanced at Maria in confusion. "Do you know what she's talking about?" she asked.

Maria shrugged. "I have no idea," she said.

Stephanie pushed aside the rest of the coats— and felt her face turn bright red.

It wasn't a cage she was pointing to. It was a locker with a wire door. Bingo wasn't behind the door, she saw now. It was only a sweater. A gray sweater with a gray fur collar.

Oops! Stephanie closed her eyes, wishing the floor would open up and swallow her. *That's it,* she thought. *It's finished. My life as a spy is over!*

She slowly opened her eyes.

"What is wrong with you?" Alexis asked. Dana stared at Stephanie with a puzzled look on her face.

"It's . . . uh, it's just that I'm totally against people wearing fur," Stephanie blurted out. "And whoever owns this sweater ought to be ashamed!"

Dana laughed. "Relax, Jane. I'm against fur coats, too. That's why this trim is *artificial* fur. See?" She lifted the sweater and handed it to Stephanie.

Stephanie read the label. It stated very plainly that no animals had been harmed to make the fur trim.

Stephanie felt herself blushing even harder. "I'm so sorry," she said.

"Don't worry about it," Dana said. "When I really believe in a cause, I get carried away, too."

"Tell me about it!" Maria rolled her eyes. "Dana really loves animals. She gets so emotional about them! We all think she should be a veterinarian."

"Really?" Stephanie smiled weakly. "That's great."

"So, if we don't see you around school, we'll see you Wednesday, right?" Dana called as she and her friends got ready to leave.

"Right. Wednesday," Stephanie promised.

She pulled on her jacket and hurried out of the bowling alley. She couldn't wait to get home. It would be a total relief not to pretend to be Jane Calzo anymore.

I just want to relax and be myself again. Stephanie sighed. She had a long way to go before she was in Great-Aunt Jane's league. Maybe a talent for spying *didn't* run in the family.

Stephanie, Darcy, and Allie walked home from school slowly on Wednesday afternoon.

"I can't wait to find out what happens tonight," Darcy remarked. "Call us the instant you get home. No matter how late it is."

"I just hope you find out something about Bingo," Allie added. "I can't believe we haven't one single clue about where he is." Allie shook her head in frustration.

Stephanie thought about how much she liked

Dana and her friends. She wondered if she could ever make Darcy and Allie understand.

"You know," Stephanie began carefully, "I'm not positive that the Kennedy kids took Bingo."

"So?" Darcy asked.

"So if they didn't take him, they wouldn't even know that he's gone," Stephanie continued.

"I don't get your point," Darcy said.

"Well, if Kennedy thinks we still have Bingo, then we still have the advantage for the game," Stephanie pointed out.

"But they *do* have him," Allie said. "I'm sure of it."

"How can you be sure?" Stephanie asked.

Allie gave her an outraged look. "Steph, whose side are you on anyway?"

"Ours, of course!" Stephanie replied. "It's just that the kids at Kennedy aren't *evil*. The ones I've met are really nice. None of them seem's like a raccoon-napper."

"Then what happened to Bingo?" Allie demanded.

"I don't know," Stephanie admitted.

"Don't argue, you guys," Darcy cut in. "Maybe Steph will learn more tonight when she paints the Kennedy bus."

"I almost wish I couldn't go," Stephanie said. "I need the time to work on my heritage report."

"Still having trouble with the research?" Darcy asked.

"Yeah. I've read all those books I took out of the library," Stephanie said. "There's not a single mention of Jane Tanner. And the project is due next week!"

"That's tough," Darcy said. "I've found out lots of great stuff. I learned that my family moved to Chicago from the South, right after the Civil War." Darcy opened her notebook and pulled out a sepia-toned photograph. "My dad had this copy made for me from the original," she said. She pointed to a tall, slender woman standing beside a horse-drawn cart. "That's my great-great-great-great-grandmother, Patience Powell."

"Patience?" Stephanie asked. "What an unusual name."

"She was born a slave," Darcy explained. "The man who owned her was a preacher who named his slaves after virtues. According to the letters she left, they all had names like Honesty, Silence, Modesty, Wisdom, and Thrift."

"That must have been one weird plantation," Allie said.

"I think all the plantations were pretty weird," Darcy said. "Imagine anyone thinking they had the right to own another person. And treat them terribly, too."

Allie shuddered. "Thank goodness my family didn't face anything like that. My family came here because they were really poor in England. My great-great-great-grandfather thought he'd have a better chance of making a living as a tailor in America."

"At least you know when your family arrived and what kind of work they did," Stephanie said. "All I've found out about Jane's family is that they came from Ireland."

"Maybe that's because Jane was a superspy," Darcy said. "Maybe all the records on her family had to be buried in Washington or something."

"Have you asked your dad about her being a spy?" Allie asked.

"Not yet," Stephanie admitted. "You know my dad. He might get so enthusiastic that he'd take over my project. Remember last year, when we had to do that history paper on San Francisco in the 1800s? He kept dragging me on walks. I think he showed me every house in the entire city that was built before the turn of the century."

"That was a little extreme," Allie agreed.

"But your dad actually knew Jane Tanner, didn't he?" Darcy reminded her.

Stephanie nodded. "Yeah. I guess I *have* to ask him."

"I think you have no choice," Allie said.

At dinner that night Stephanie decided to take the plunge. "Uh, Dad," she began hesitantly, "remember when I asked you about Great-Aunt Jane? Well, I'm wondering if there was anything *extra* you didn't tell me about her."

"Not a thing," her father said.

"That's funny," Joey joked. "That's exactly what I remember about her. Not a thing! Do you think that's because I never met her?"

Stephanie groaned. Joey could be pretty funny. But now she needed information, not jokes.

D.J. caught a glass just as Nicky tipped it over. "Really, Dad," she said. "I'm curious, too. I always thought Great-Aunt Jane was a teacher."

"Yup," Danny replied. "She was."

"You must remember more than that," Stephanie said.

"I remember my parents taking me to visit her when I was a kid," Danny said. "She looked a lot like you, Steph. Except that she was taller and her hair was darker."

"And?" Stephanie prompted.

Her father thought a moment. "I remember she got angry at me once for vacuuming her dog. And another time she was mad at me for pouring all the salt out of her salt shaker. I was doing this trick, where you balance the shaker on its edge—"

"I never could get that trick to work," Joey said.

"Really? I did," Danny said. "Here, I'll show you how." Danny and Joey huddled over the salt shaker.

"This is not helping," Stephanie muttered.

Jesse handed Alex a piece of bread, then looked at her curiously. "What kind of help do you need, Steph?" he asked.

"Just more information," she said. "You see, I already know that Great-Aunt Jane was a spy in World War Two, and—"

Danny dropped the salt shaker. "Aunt Jane? A spy?" He laughed. "No way! She was a schoolteacher."

"But I have proof. Wait—I'll show you." Stephanie ran to her room. A few minutes later she returned with the newspaper photograph. She handed it to her dad.

"*Jane Tanner, World War Two Spy*," he read aloud. "Wow!" His voice was awed. "An aunt of mine was actually a spy. This is incredible, Steph! All those years, I never guessed that Aunt Jane once led a secret life."

"Hold on, Dad," D.J. said. "This isn't enough information to prove that Great-Aunt Jane was a spy."

"It isn't enough information to write a decent report, either," Stephanie complained.

Her father was thoughtful. "Maybe not. But I know you'll get the real story, Steph."

Not at this rate, Stephanie thought.

"Let me know how your research goes," Danny went on. "I can't wait to learn more about my family. I never dreamed anyone I'm related to was this exciting. Maybe we could all go to the library tonight. We could leave right after dinner," he suggested.

"Uh, no, I can't," Stephanie said. She glanced at her watch. She had just enough time to get to Kennedy for the bus-decorating party.

"Why not?" her dad asked.

"Because . . ." Stephanie hesitated. She didn't want to lie to her father. She felt as if she'd been doing nothing *but* lying lately. But she had to. It was part of her cover. "Well, because I have to go to Allie's to work on math," she finally said.

Danny looked crushed. "Oh. Well, we'll just have to go some other time," he said.

"Sure, Dad. No problem." Stephanie excused herself from the table and hurried upstairs to change her clothes.

She wanted to feel like Jane Calzo when she went to Kennedy. Moments later Stephanie gazed into the mirror. She'd changed from leggings and a sweater to overalls and a long-sleeved T-shirt. After all, it was a painting party.

I wonder if Great-Aunt Jane hated lying all the time? Stephanie thought as she headed down the stairs. *I guess it's part of the job. This spy business is harder than I thought. But it's worth all the problems—if I can track down Bingo.*

CHAPTER
9

◆ ◢ ◣ ◆

It was almost dark by the time Stephanie reached Kennedy Middle School. The parking lot was brightly lit both by electric lights and a full moon in the sky. In the very center of the parking lot was a bright yellow bus surrounded by kids. Ladders had been leaned up against the bus.

Some kids were busy painting posters. Others braided crepe-paper streamers. Still others were putting the finishing touches on a giant cardboard Coyote. The Coyote wore a basketball uniform. His expression was challenging and he was flexing his muscles. Even Stephanie had to admit he was pretty cute.

"Hi, Jane!" Dana called out from the top of

the bus. For an instant, Stephanie forgot that *she* was Jane. "Hey, Jane," Dana yelled. "Over here."

Stephanie looked around. Where was this Jane that Dana was calling to. Then it hit her. *She* was Jane!

"Oh—hi," she called back.

Dana and Sherri were wrapping the bars of the luggage rack in orange and silver streamers—the Kennedy colors.

"Jane, hi." Billy stepped out of the crowd. He hurried up to Stephanie. A wide smile spread across his face. "Want to help with the posters?"

"Sure," Stephanie replied. She couldn't help smiling back. There was something so *nice* about Billy. She walked beside him through the parking lot.

"So, where have you been hiding all week?" he asked her. "I kept looking for you. I checked all three lunch periods in the cafeteria. But I didn't see you anywhere."

Oops! Stephanie thought. She'd rehearsed all sorts of answers to questions that the Kennedy kids might ask. But somehow she hadn't counted on being asked why no one actually saw her *in* the school.

"Uh, I was out this week," she fibbed.

"Were you sick?" Billy asked. He seemed genuinely worried.

"No, I'm fine," Stephanie said. She thought quickly. "There was some trouble with my great-aunt."

"Was she sick?" Billy asked.

"Uh, yeah. Really sick," Stephanie replied. "Actually, she died." *More than ten years ago*, she added to herself.

"Did you have to go to the funeral?" Billy asked.

Stephanie blinked. "Right. The funeral. Well, yeah, that's why I wasn't in school. We had to drive down to San Diego for the funeral. We just got back a couple of hours ago."

Stephanie couldn't believe the stories she was telling. It was a good thing she was a writer—with an active imagination.

Billy touched her shoulder. "I'm really sorry. That must have been rough."

"Well, Great-Aunt Jane was an amazing woman," Stephanie said.

Billy nodded. "Well, you're probably glad to be back."

"Definitely!" Stephanie said. "And ready to work. How are you going to keep this dry for a week and a half?" she asked, pointing to the decorated bus.

"We're putting it in a garage," Billy answered. "Under wraps. Kind of our secret weapon for beating Muir."

Stephanie then turned toward the big piece of poster board that lay on the painting tables. Someone had already stenciled in the words COY-OTES RULE!

Billy handed Stephanie a paintbrush. "Here you go," he said. "Just try to stay within the lines," he joked.

"No problem." Stephanie dipped her brush into a jar of neon-orange paint and began filling in the lettering. She couldn't believe she was helping the Coyotes. For a moment, she felt like a total traitor.

"You know, I had an amazing great-aunt, too," Billy remarked. "She started a woman's softball league. We have a lot of pictures of her, swinging a baseball bat and looking totally fierce. My dad says that's where all the athletic genes in our family come from."

"That is so cool!" Stephanie said.

Billy smiled. "Well, my mom isn't too keen on our family history. She's not even sure what country her ancestors came from. Can you believe it? She always says, 'Don't worry about the past. Just concentrate on the present.'"

"I wish she'd tell that to my history teacher," Stephanie joked.

"I bet," Billy said. He frowned. "So, who *do* you have for—" he began to ask.

Oh, no! What have I done! Stephanie panicked.

Billy was about to ask who her history teacher was. And she hadn't a clue what she should answer.

Quick—say something! Anything! Just change the subject, she ordered herself. But her mind was a complete blank.

She plunged her brush into the paint jar and pulled it out quickly, purposely spattering orange paint all over the ground.

"Oh, no. I totally spilled paint everywhere!" she exclaimed.

"Hey, it's okay. It's only the parking lot," Billy told her, forgetting all about her history teacher. "And at least you didn't spill it *on* anyone."

Stephanie breathed a sigh of relief. *That was way too close*, she told herself. *I have to be more careful.*

She took a deep breath to calm down. She and Billy worked silently for a while. Stephanie found herself wishing she could forget about being a spy. Billy was so nice, and so easy to be with. As she painted, she found herself imagining what it would be like to go out with him.

Stop it! she ordered herself. *Don't even think that way. He won't want to go out with you—not after he finds out the truth—that you're Stephanie Tanner from John Muir—not Jane Calzo from Kennedy.*

But that thought only made her feel worse.

She really liked Billy. And all she'd done was feed him her cover story since they met.

Dana and Sherri scrambled down the ladder from the roof of the bus. They walked up to Stephanie just as Scott called Billy over to check out his poster.

"Hey, Jane. How's it going?" Sherri asked.

"Good," Stephanie replied.

"How come I didn't see you in school this week?" Dana asked.

Stephanie repeated the story about her great-aunt's death.

"That's so sad. I'm really sorry," Dana told her.

"Yeah. Well, thanks," Stephanie muttered. Great. Now she felt even guiltier. Dana could be a good friend, Stephanie felt. But she had deceived her, too.

"Hey, I just remembered. Didn't you say you have Ms. Dolan for English?" Sherri asked.

Stephanie thought back to the newspaper article Allie had found. "Yeah. Ms. Dolan," she replied.

"I thought so. I have her, too, first period," Sherri said. "You must be in her third-period class. Listen, since you were out, do you want me to lend you my notes for the last three days?"

"I—I—that'd be great," Stephanie said. How could she refuse?

Now Sherri would try to arrange a way for Stephanie to pick up the notes, and then a way to return them. Which meant Stephanie would have to come up with more lies about why she couldn't meet Sherri before, during, or after school.

All that, and she wasn't learning anything about Bingo, which was the whole point of her being there in the first place!

Think, Steph encouraged herself. How do I casually bring up a stolen raccoon?

"Uh, Sherri," Stephanie began before Sherri or Dana could continue the conversation. "I was wondering. Uh, actually, my dad was asking me about the neighborhood. Are there many . . . *thefts?*"

"Not that I know of," Sherri replied. "I think some grocery store was broken into a couple of years ago. But this neighborhood is pretty quiet."

"Well, it's really our dog that my dad is worried about," Stephanie went on. "He heard there's been a series of pet-nappings around here."

Dana's eyebrows rose in surprise. "I never heard *anything* like that," she said.

"Sometimes I think my dad just likes to worry," Stephanie said. "You know how weird parents can be."

"Do I!" Dana exclaimed. "That's the whole reason I still use my tree house. Just to have some space where—" Dana flushed.

"Where what?" Stephanie asked.

"Nothing," Dana said.

"No, really," Stephanie said with a burst of curiosity. "What were you saying about your tree house?"

Dana seemed embarrassed. "It's just that saying I have a tree house sounds so dumb. It makes me feel like I'm ten."

"No, it doesn't," Stephanie assured her. "I think it sounds really cool. I'd love to have a place to escape from my family once in a while."

"Really? You know, my dad built it when I was eight," Dana explained. "But this year I started fixing it up." She grinned. "I actually had to raise the roof. I kept bumping my head."

Stephanie laughed. Scott, who had been eavesdropping, turned around and tugged on Dana's hair. "So when am I going to get to see this famous tree house?" he asked.

"I told you, it's off limits to guys," Dana said.

"Now, *that* sounds like you're ten," Scott teased.

"I need a place where I can get some peace," Dana teased back. "I see more than enough of you in school."

"Does that mean you don't want to go to the dance with me Friday night?" Scott pretended to be hurt.

"I'll let you know." Dana smiled.

Scott gave her a low bow. "Thank you, your highness. I humbly await your answer."

Dana threw a roll of crepe paper at him, then turned back to Stephanie. "Hey, Jane, what about you? Are you going to the dance Friday?"

"That's exactly what I was wondering," Billy said. Stephanie turned and found him standing right behind her.

Stephanie froze. "Dance? Friday?" She knew

she couldn't answer questions for a whole evening about her fake self. "I—I can't," she finally said.

"Why not?" Billy asked.

"Because . . ." Stephanie wondered just how many stories she should tell in one night. Should she say she already had a date for Friday?

But then Billy would think she had a boyfriend. And she didn't want him to think that.

Things were getting so complicated!

"Because I'm going back down to San Diego on Friday," Stephanie blurted out. "To help my family clean out my great-aunt's house and stuff."

"Oh, bummer," Billy said. His smile faded from his face.

"Yeah," Stephanie agreed. Suddenly she pictured herself dancing with Billy, laughing and having a great time. Maybe even kissing him goodnight. "It's a major bummer," she said.

She felt even worse as she rode the city bus home from Kennedy that evening. She liked Billy more and more, and he really seemed to like her. He was so incredibly easy to talk to. And she loved the way his eyes crinkled up when he laughed.

She sighed. She also liked Dana and Sherri. In

fact, she hadn't met anyone she *didn't* like. They all felt like friends. It was getting harder and harder to pretend to be someone she wasn't when she was around them.

It was so much easier for Great-Aunt Jane, she thought. She had been spying for her country during a world war. That was a clear-cut case of good against evil. Jane Tanner knew who the enemy was.

Kennedy is the enemy, she reminded herself. *They're John Muir's biggest rival.*

Somehow, though, these kids didn't feel like the enemy.

Stephanie's mind raced. What if the kids at Kennedy hadn't taken Bingo? She was finding it harder and harder to believe that any of them would kidnap a raccoon.

Stephanie got off the bus and walked slowly toward her house. But if the Kennedy kids *didn't* take Bingo, then who did? Or did he really just escape? And if he did, would they ever be able to find him?

"Stephanie Tanner, do you realize what time it is?"

Stephanie jumped at the sound of her father's voice. Her dad was standing in the doorway of their house, looking worried—and angry!

He pointed to his watch. "It's after nine-thirty. *On a week night.* You know you're not allowed to be out this late!"

"I'm sorry," Stephanie said. "We were talking a bit after we studied and I lost track of the time."

"Okay. That's understandable," Danny said. "But couldn't you have taken two minutes to call, when you realized how late it was, and let me know you were okay?"

"I'm sorry, Dad." Stephanie hung her head. "I just totally wasn't thinking."

"Well, maybe you'll remember when you're taking Comet out for his walk all this week." Danny frowned. "And next week, too."

"Dad, that's not fair!" Stephanie protested.

"Would you like to be grounded as well?" he asked.

"No," she said quickly. "I have too much spying—I mean, too much research to do. At the library."

"Fine. Then you're walking Comet." Danny dropped a kiss on the top of her head. "Now go inside and get some sleep. It's late."

Stephanie's feet felt heavy as she trudged up to her room. Great. Now she had to be home to walk Comet every night. And she was no closer to finding Bingo than she ever was. So far, she had to admit—she was a total bust as a spy. She hadn't found out anything useful about Bingo. And the big game with Kennedy was just over a week away!

CHAPTER
10

◆ ◢ ◾ ◆

"I can't believe it's Thursday already," Stephanie complained. She frowned at Darcy and Allie as they hurried toward the public library after school. "I still need to finish my heritage project!"

"Don't you mean you still have to spy around and find Bingo?" Allie asked.

"That, too," Stephanie said. She paused. "Though I'm beginning to think we were all wrong about that."

"What do you mean?" Allie demanded.

"I just mean, it *is* possible that the Kennedy kids *didn't* steal Bingo," Stephanie said.

"Are you serious?" Darcy asked. "Of course they did. Kennedy is the enemy!"

"The kids I know at Kennedy don't feel like enemies. Not now that I'm getting to know them," Stephanie said. "Even the guys on the basketball team are pretty cool."

Darcy narrowed her eyes. "It sounds to me like our spy has her sides mixed up."

"I do not," Stephanie protested.

"But they stole Bingo. I know they did," Allie insisted.

"Listen, Allie," Stephanie began to explain. "I know you want to believe that Bingo was kidnapped. Because if he just disappeared, well, you know, maybe we'd *never* find him."

"What are you saying?" Allie asked.

"Just that you might *need* to think he's kidnapped," Stephanie went on. "Because then he'd be safer, in a way. I mean, I know how much you love him and all. I know you can't bear to think of him being out there, hurt. Or hit by a car, or—"

"Stop!" Allie covered her ears.

"You might have a point, Steph," Darcy admitted. "But you haven't uncovered any proof that Kennedy *didn't* steal Bingo, either. So what's your next step?"

"I don't know," Stephanie replied. "One of the

guys on their team invited me to a dance Friday night, but—"

"You're dating a Coyote now?" Allie asked.

"No. I said I couldn't go," Stephanie finished.

"Why not?" Darcy asked. "That's perfect. I mean, that's a trick used by all the great female spies in history. They made enemy agents fall in love with them. Then the agents spilled all their secrets to them. It's totally romantic. It's what Mata Hari would have done!"

"Mata Hari wound up getting shot by a firing squad," Stephanie reminded her.

"True," Darcy said. "But that won't happen to you."

Stephanie found herself slowing down as the library came into sight. "Maybe I'm not cut out to be one of the great female spies of history," she admitted. "Billy is sweet and funny, and I like talking to him. Lying to him is *not* romantic, and totally not cool."

Allie stared at her in shock. "You *really* like him," she said accusingly.

"Maybe," Stephanie said. "I keep thinking how he'll feel if he finds out my name isn't Jane Calzo. If he finds out everything he knows about me is untrue."

Darcy sat down on the library steps. She gave

Stephanie a penetrating look. "Let me get this straight," she said. "You have a crush on a Coyote."

"Look, this isn't just about Billy," Stephanie said, sitting down beside Darcy. "I'm kind of friendly with a girl named Dana. She's really gone out of her way to make me feel welcome. She's great. I mean, you guys would really like her if she went to John Muir. I don't like lying to her *or* to Billy. To any of them, really."

"Does that mean you're giving up on being a spy?" Allie asked.

A cool wind blew across the library steps. Stephanie pulled her hooded sweatshirt from her pack and slipped it on. "No. But I don't know how much longer I can keep it up," she replied. "I can barely remember what lies I told to everyone. Every time I see the kids from Kennedy, I have to make up fifty new stories on the spot—why no one's ever seen me take a class there, why I can't go to the dance . . ." Stephanie dropped her head into her hands. "And now they all think I have a great-aunt in San Diego who just died!"

"Wow!" Darcy tried not to laugh. "I see what you mean. I guess this spy business isn't very easy."

"But what about Bingo?" Allie asked, her voice trembling. "We can't give up on him."

"I know, and I don't want to," Stephanie said. "But, honestly, I haven't found a single clue that shows that the Kennedy kids took him."

"Maybe you have," Darcy said.

Stephanie raised her head. "What?"

"Well, I read a lot of mystery stories," Darcy explained. "And a lot of times, I'm halfway through the book and the detective doesn't realize she already has the clue that she needs to solve the case. It's not until later that all the pieces fall into place. So maybe you already have the clue to Bingo's disappearance and you just don't realize it."

"Maybe," Stephanie said.

"Darcy could be right. You need to think back on all your conversations with the Kennedy kids," Allie said. "Did anyone ever say anything suspicious?"

"Not really," Stephanie replied.

"What about this guy Billy?" Darcy asked. "Did he tell you anything about their basketball team?"

"Not very much," Stephanie admitted. She looked up. "Speaking of basketball teams . . ." she said. Josh and Rob Hernandez were walking toward the library. Rob was the Raccoons' point guard.

"They must be working on their heritage reports, too," Darcy said.

Josh reached the steps first.

"Hey, how's it going?" Darcy asked him. "Are the Raccoons ready to beat the shorts off Kennedy?"

Josh shook his head. "It doesn't look good. The guys are still shaken up about Bingo disappearing."

"With Bingo gone, our winning streak might be gone, too," Rob added. "Not that we're giving up . . . I mean, if we don't find Bingo, we're going to have to figure out some new rituals for luck—"

Darcy's eyebrows shot up. "What kind of rituals?"

"We're talking about shaving our heads before the game," Josh said.

Stephanie winced. "You've got to be kidding!"

"Nope," both boys said at once.

Stephanie pictured Josh, her friend, with a shaved head.

Yikes! I have to find that raccoon, she thought. *And fast!*

"Well, we all have research to do," Rob said. "So I guess we'd better get started."

Stephanie, Darcy, and Allie followed the boys into the library. Stephanie went straight to the computer database. She'd already checked out every book and magazine on spies. But she still hadn't found a thing about her great-aunt Jane. Today she was determined to change that.

She started looking under the category *World War II.* She groaned. There were over five hundred books in the library system on World War II. Of course, not all of them would be at her branch. She hit the button that would list the first five book titles. It was going to be a very long night.

Forty minutes later, her vision was blurry. So far she'd scrolled through nearly twenty screens of data. She'd read every summary of any book about World War II spies, but none of the summaries mentioned Jane Tanner.

This is crazy, Stephanie thought. *Didn't spies ever write their memoirs?*

She sighed and called up the next screen. *Famous Battles of World War II. Famous Fighter Planes of World War II. Famous Generals of World War II . . .*

Then she found it. *The Secret Lives of Little-*

Known World War II Spies. If any book would have information about Great-Aunt Jane, this would be the one!

Stephanie checked the call number. There was a copy of the book in this branch of the library, but someone had checked it out. It figured.

Stephanie wrote down the title, the author, and the Dewey decimal number that told where the book was shelved. She brought the information to Ms. Craven at the main desk.

"Can you tell me when this book should be returned?" Stephanie asked.

"I'll check the computer," Ms. Craven said. "We'll see when it's supposed to come back. If you like, I can reserve it for you and call you when it comes in."

"That would be great," Stephanie said. "I just hope it comes in soon."

Stephanie watched as Ms. Craven clicked the mouse on her computer. On the screen Stephanie scanned a list of books that were recently checked out. "Wait—stop right there!" she suddenly ordered.

"Here?" Ms. Craven looked up in surprise. "But this isn't the right list for your book. These books are about caring for animals."

"Actually, I also need some books on that subject," Stephanie told her.

"Which book did you need?" Ms. Craven asked.

"Those," Stephanie replied, pointing to an entry. "The ones on wild raccoons."

Ms. Craven clicked the mouse again. A screen appeared showing the name of the person who checked out the books and the date they were due back.

"Well, you're out of luck," Ms. Craven said. "These books aren't due back for another week."

"Oh, I'm not out of luck," Stephanie murmured, staring at the screen. "I just found exactly what I need."

Ms. Craven gazed at her curiously. Stephanie's mind was reeling. According to Ms. Craven's list, all the books on raccoon care were checked out by one person. A person Stephanie knew.

A person named Dana Pugnosian.

CHAPTER
11

♦ ◂ ◂ ♦

Stephanie couldn't believe it. This was it. The clue she needed. Dana *must* have Bingo. Why else would she be checking out books on raccoon care? It couldn't be a coincidence—could it?

"The other book you wanted is due back at this branch next Monday," Ms. Craven said. "Stephanie? Did you hear me?"

"Wh-what?" Stephanie blinked.

"The Secret Lives of Little-Known Spies of World War Two," Ms. Craven reminded her.

"Oh, right," Stephanie said.

Ms. Craven handed her a form. "Fill out this request," she said. "We'll call you as soon as the book comes in."

Stephanie filled out the form. She could barely think about her research on Great-Aunt Jane. She had to find Dana.

She had to know what was going on!

Stephanie rushed out of the library without saying good-bye to her friends. She headed for the bus stop.

I'll try Valdi's first, she decided. *If Dana isn't there, maybe someone else from Kennedy will know where to find her.*

Twenty minutes later Stephanie peered through Valdi's window. It wasn't nearly so crowded as the first time she had been there. She didn't see Billy or any of the guys on the team, but she did spot Dana. She was sitting with Laura and Sherri in a booth in the back of the restaurant.

Stephanie crossed her fingers. *Time for a little bit of cloak-and-dagger work,* she told herself.

She pulled up the hood on her sweatshirt so that it covered her hair and most of her face. It wasn't much of a disguise, but it was the best she could do.

The booth directly behind Dana's was empty. Stephanie walked quickly over to it. She slid onto the seat and then slumped down slowly until she was lying flat. If anyone asked, she'd say she'd dropped a contact lens and was look-ing for it on the floor.

She felt sweat trickling down her chest. It was hot in the restaurant, especially with her hood pulled up over her head. The seat of the booth was sticky with someone's spilled soda.

Yuck, she thought. *This is definitely not the kind of glamorous spying that Great-Aunt Jane did!*

Then again, even Great-Aunt Jane must have had an uncomfortable moment or two, she realized.

Stephanie concentrated on the conversation in the booth behind her. It wasn't easy to hear. The pizza parlor was noisy. The guy behind the counter was calling out orders to the pizza chef. Ace of Bass was blaring their latest hit on the jukebox. A bunch of guys in the booth near Stephanie were boasting about how much pizza they could eat. And Dana and her friends weren't talking particularly loudly.

Stephanie strained to pick out the girls' voices.

"So how's he doing?" Sherri asked.

"Great," Dana said. "His leg is much better now."

"I hope he's totally better for the big game," Laura said.

"Me, too," Dana replied. "I really want him to be there. He's so cute!"

Stephanie frowned. Were they talking about

Bingo? Or about a basketball player? Their conversation could apply to a raccoon—or a boy.

"We could stop at your house on our way home today," Laura said. "Will he be there?"

Dana giggled. "I'll make sure he is," she said.

"Great," Sherri replied. "Wow! Look at the time." Stephanie could picture her checking her watch. "I'm supposed to be home in an hour," she said. "We'd better leave now."

"No problem," Dana said. "Let's just finish our pizza and go."

Their conversation stopped for a few minutes. Then the girls started chatting and laughing as they got ready to leave.

Stephanie slipped down to the floor as Dana and her friends stood up. She could hear them zipping their jackets and dropping coins on the table for a tip. She crouched closer to the bottom of the booth with her face turned to the wall. If anyone looked, all they would see was someone in jeans and a sweatshirt.

Looking for a contact lens, Stephanie reminded herself. Still, she was shaking. *Please, please, don't let them notice me*, she chanted. *Please don't let anyone notice me.*

She heard the girls head out of the restaurant. She counted to fifty, then slid out from under the table. She hurried to the door and flew through the entrance. Outside, she looked both ways, up and down the street.

Dana and her friends had gone to the right and were already at the end of the block, turning the corner. Stephanie hurried after them. Now all she had to do was follow them to Dana's— without being seen.

Stephanie crossed to the other side of the street and kept a good distance between herself and the Kennedy girls. Every time one of them turned her head, Stephanie ducked into a doorway. Once, she was sure that Laura stared directly at her. She froze and held her breath. A moment later, though, Laura turned to Sherri, laughing about something. The girls continued walking. Stephanie gave a sigh of relief and trailed them again.

After that she actually started to enjoy herself. She felt like a true spy. It was probably no accident that she was the one who found out about Great-Aunt Jane. Obviously, she had inherited Jane's talent for espionage.

All these years Stephanie had thought she wanted to be a writer when she grew up. Maybe she'd be a writer *and* a spy. She could write bestselling spy novels based on her experiences. She could . . .

Stephanie came to a sudden halt. Dana and her friends had gone into a small store that sold newspapers and candy. Stephanie hung back, waiting for them. Minutes went by. She tapped her foot impatiently.

They were probably just buying some gum, she told herself. Or making a phone call. They'd be out any second. She glanced at her watch. Five minutes had passed. What if they knew she was following them and ducked out a back entrance? What if she'd lost them completely?

Just as that thought occurred to her, the girls hurried out of the store. Dana was the third one through the door. To Stephanie's horror, Dana glanced right in her direction. Instantly, Stephanie dove behind a car. Had Dana seen her?

"What in the world are you doing?" asked a familiar voice.

Stephanie felt her heart thud. It couldn't be.

"Jane, are you all right? Jane?" the voice asked.

Slowly Stephanie stood up—and gazed directly into Billy's worried eyes.

CHAPTER
12

◆ ◀ ◆ ◆

"I saw you hiding out here," Billy said. "Are you in trouble? Is someone after you?"

Stephanie considered saying yes. But if she told Billy that someone *was* after her, he just might try to be a hero or something.

"No, uh—I was looking for my contact lens," she blurted out. "It popped out of my eye."

"Oh. I'll help you look," Billy offered.

"No, I already found it," Stephanie said. "I was just kneeling down to put it back in." She blinked several times. "There. All set."

"Great." Billy looked relieved. "So, do you want to go to Valdi's and get some pizza?"

"Thanks, but I just came from there," Stephanie told him. "I'm full." She glanced down the street. Dana, Laura, and Sherri were hurrying away from the newsstand. They were almost out of sight. She had to get rid of Billy before she lost them!

Billy studied her curiously. "Why do you have your hood up? It's not that cold out."

Stephanie felt a sudden burst of inspiration. "Actually, I think I'm coming down with a cold," she said. "My little sister was sick last week, and now I've got the chills and—" She sneezed loudly. "You know—if you've got that big game coming up, you probably should steer clear of me for a while." She sneezed again and threw in a cough for good measure.

Billy took a step back from her. "You're really having a rough time," he said, frowning sympathetically. "I feel like I ought to bring you chicken soup or something."

"Don't do that," she said. "Just keep your distance."

"Right." Billy grinned. "The guys on the team would kill me if I got sick before the game with John Muir."

Stephanie sniffed and tried to look pathetic. "It's okay," she said. "I understand."

"I hope you're better in time to watch the game," Billy said.

"I plan to be," Stephanie told him.

"Okay, then. I guess we'll talk," Billy said.

Stephanie nodded. "Okay. I'd better get home and get to bed. My throat's pretty sore."

"Take care of yourself," Billy called.

"I will," Stephanie promised.

As soon as Billy was gone, Stephanie raced in the direction Dana and the others had gone. But her mind was on Billy. No guy had ever even *thought* of bringing her chicken soup before!

He was just so sweet. She felt a stab of dread as she thought about the talk they would have to have—after the big game.

How did I ever get myself into this? Stephanie sighed. She didn't want to be cruel to Billy. But she had to be loyal to her own friends first. Allie, Darcy, Josh, the John Muir basketball team—everyone was counting on her.

It was too late for regrets now. She couldn't turn back when she was so close to finding Bingo.

A block and a half later Stephanie caught sight of Dana again. She and her friends had turned off the street and were walking toward a tall white Victorian house. The roof was edged with lacy gingerbread trim. A shingle that hung above the mailbox read PUGNOSIAN.

Stephanie hesitated as the girls walked toward the front door.

How will I explain showing up at Dana's without an invitation? she asked herself.

To her relief, the girls didn't climb the flight of stairs that led to the front door. Instead, they took a path along the side of the house.

Stephanie counted to fifty before following them. She pressed herself flat against the side of the house and inched toward the backyard. She could hear their voices. She reached the back edge of the house.

Stephanie peeked out. She could see a long, rectangular grassy lawn edged with flower beds. There was one tall oak tree at the very back of the property. A ladder led up into its branches—and into the biggest tree house she had ever seen.

Dana and the others climbed the ladder. Stephanie hesitated before stepping into the yard. Should she confront Dana and her friends now? Or should she get help? She could run back to a phone booth and call Allie and Darcy. Or maybe she should . . .

"Jane," Dana called out.

Oops! Stephanie raised her head and forced herself to smile.

Dana leaned out of the tree house. "Hey," she called in a friendly voice. "What are you doing here?"

Here we go again, Stephanie thought. *Time to invent another story. Fast!*

"I—um, I realized I *did* need help making up those English classes I missed," she said. "One of the kids at Valdi's told me you were all over here, so I came to see if I could borrow your notes."

"Of course you can borrow my notes," Dana said. She nodded toward the tree house. "My notebook is up here in my pack." She looked thoughtful for a moment. Sherri and Laura poked their heads out of the tree house, too, and Dana glanced at them. They nodded.

"Do you want to come up?" Dana finally asked.

"Sure," Stephanie said. Carefully, she climbed the ladder and entered the tree house. "This is amazing," she said. "It feels just like a little house."

A braided rug covered the floor. Four small upholstered chairs were clustered around a table in the center of the room. A bright red bookshelf was stuffed with paperbacks. Photographs were hung over all the walls. Most of them were pictures of wild animals.

Dana had set up a desk and chair against one wall. Stephanie glanced at it. On top of the desk was a big metal pet cage. And in the cage—Stephanie gasped—in the cage was Bingo!

Stephanie felt a chill run down the length of her spine. She was happy and sad at the same time. She found Bingo! It was thrilling. She was a *great* spy!

Now she knew that her new friends weren't so nice after all. They were raccoon-nappers!

Dana was looking at her as if she expected Stephanie to say something.

Stephanie blurted out the first thing that came into her mind. "Wow! That's a real raccoon!"

"Yup. He's real, all right," Dana said.

"I never knew anyone with a pet raccoon before," Stephanie told her. "Um, have you had him long?"

"Well, he's not really mine," Dana answered. "Actually, he *was* John Muir's."

Stephanie fought to keep her voice casual. "What do you mean?" she asked.

Dana explained how Bingo was John Muir's team's mascot.

"I don't get it," Stephanie said. "You mean you stole Bingo from John Muir so they'd lose the big game to Kennedy?"

"Huh?" Dana stared at her. "No," she finally said. "This has nothing to do with the game."

"Oh, sure. Right." Stephanie smiled as if they were sharing a joke.

"No, really," Dana insisted. "We stole Bingo because he shouldn't be spending his life in a cage."

Sherri and Laura nodded in agreement.

"But you have him in a cage," Stephanie pointed out.

"Only to keep him safe until his foot's healed," Dana said. "And it seems fine now."

"That's right," Sherri agreed. "We had to be certain Bingo could survive in the wild again. Because we're going to set him free."

"You are?" Stephanie stared at her in amazement.

"You bet. It's just dumb that John Muir thinks Bingo is the secret to their winning streak. I mean, what if they *never* let him go? Bingo needs to be set free," Sherri continued.

Stephanie swallowed hard. It never occurred to her that there might be another reason for taking Bingo. Something besides winning the basketball game. Dana wanted to *help* Bingo. She loved animals as much as Allie did. Maybe more!

"Does the Kennedy team know you have Bingo?" Stephanie asked.

"No way!" Dana answered.

"If they found out, they'd probably want to use him to get back at John Muir," Sherri replied. She shook her head in disgust.

"Wow," Stephanie said. "I know you're all loyal to the Coyotes. And you care about the game, too. But you care even more about Bingo."

"Of course," Dana said. "Bingo can't help himself, can he? It's up to us to take care of animals."

"Right," Laura agreed.

Dana's eyes met Stephanie's. "No one except us knows we have Bingo. You have to swear to keep our secret, Jane."

Stephanie gulped. The whole point of her spying was to find out Dana's secret—and then tell her friends at John Muir. Suddenly Stephanie felt like a giant rat.

"Jane, you're not swearing," Sherri said.

"Well . . ." Stephanie stalled. She glanced at Bingo, who was busily cleaning his fur. "It's just that I want to be completely fair. And it seems to me that the John Muir kids must be pretty attached to Bingo, too," she said.

"That's probably true," Dana admitted. "He is lovable. But he's not a domesticated animal, like a cat or a dog. He shouldn't be kept in a house. You never can be sure that a wild animal will act tame. His survival instincts could surface. He could get scared and then bite or attack someone."

"She's right," Sherri said. "Besides, keeping him in a cage is like keeping him in prison. Bingo needs to be in the wild, and we're going to take him there."

"Will you keep our secret?" Dana asked.

Stephanie's head was spinning with confusion. She wasn't sure whom to betray. Allie was counting on her. So was Josh. And all of John Muir cared about the big game. How would they ever win without their mascot? The John Muir students really loved Bingo, and Dana stole him from them.

On the other hand, Dana obviously cared about Bingo, too. Enough to rescue him from John Muir.

Deep down, Stephanie felt that Dana was right. A wild animal should be allowed to live in the wild. Maybe the John Muir kids *were* being selfish. She remembered how Allie had talked about setting Bingo free once his leg was healed, but then as the time grew closer she made excuses to keep him.

"What's your answer, Jane?" Dana was watching her closely. "Are you with us?"

"Yes," Stephanie said. She couldn't help it. She agreed with everything Dana and her friends were saying.

"Great! Then you can come and help us release him!" Dana's eyes were shining in anticipation.

"Release him?" Stephanie swallowed hard.

"Definitely." Dana looked straight at Stephanie. "Bingo becomes a free raccoon Saturday morning at ten. Now that you know our secret, we want you to come with us."

Stephanie smiled even though she felt sick to her stomach. "I'll be there," she promised.

CHAPTER
13

◆ ◢ ◣ ◆

"No! Not another foul!" Stephanie groaned.

She shook her head in frustration. The John Muir basketball team was in the middle of their Friday afternoon practice. They had only one week left till the Muir–Kennedy game, and they were playing terribly.

The ball kept flying out of bounds. The players kept fouling. And no one could hit a jump shot to save his life. The writing was on the wall. The team needed a miracle to turn their game around. Otherwise, John Muir was definitely going to lose.

And it will be my fault, Stephanie thought. She could tell them where to find Bingo. The team could have their mascot back, and they could have good luck in time for the game. The whole future of the John Muir basketball team was completely in her hands. And she felt paralyzed. She had no idea what to do.

She left the gym and walked slowly home. How did real spies cope? Did they get stuck in such complicated situations?

They probably never stuck around long enough to feel so torn, Stephanie decided. If she were a real spy, she would just request a new case. Some daring new mission—in a country on the other side of the globe!

"I'm home," Stephanie called as she entered her house.

"In here," Joey answered from the kitchen. Stephanie dragged her feet as she pushed through the swinging door. She was startled to find Allie and Darcy sitting with Joey. They were helping him sort a huge mountain of junk mail. In front of them were three piles labeled SAVE, MAYBE, and TOSS.

"Dumb!" Allie threw an ad for fake fingernails in the pile labeled TOSS.

"Interesting," Darcy remarked, scanning an ad for a self-cleaning cat box.

"Are you kidding? Definitely the TOSS pile,"

Joey directed her. "We don't have a cat. But this—" He grinned at Stephanie. "What would you say to a 'Perfect Summer Safari Helmet' that has a little fan inside to keep your head cool? It costs only $125.99."

"Honestly? I'd say it would make you look like a complete dweeb," Stephanie answered.

"Exactly what I thought," Joey said, throwing the ad onto the TOSS pile.

Darcy stood up. "Where have you been?" she asked Stephanie.

"What do you mean?" Stephanie asked.

"I mean, we all agreed to meet here after school today," Darcy reminded her.

Stephanie winced. "Sorry, I totally forgot! I stayed to watch the Raccoons' basketball practice," she said.

"How were they today?" Darcy asked, looking nervous.

"Pathetic," Stephanie answered. "I've never seen them play so badly. If you could even call it playing. It was like they forgot where the basket was."

"I knew it!" Darcy groaned.

"It's Bingo," Allie declared, shaking her head. "It's because he's still missing."

"Do you have any news, Steph?" Darcy gave her a hopeful look.

"Well, yeah. Let's go up to my room," Stephanie suggested.

"Excuse me," Joey spoke up. "But are you really going to make me sort through this junk mail on my own?"

"Yes," Darcy and Allie answered together.

Joey looked upset until he saw Michelle coming down the stairs. "Michelle," he called out. "I could really use your help in here."

Stephanie led Allie and Darcy up the back stairs. She walked into the bedroom she shared with Michelle and sighed. As usual, Michelle's clothes had appeared on Stephanie's bed.

Stephanie lifted a pile of grubby sweatclothes and flung it over Michelle's desk chair. Then she sprawled out on her own bed. Allie sat at Stephanie's desk. Darcy squeezed herself between the large stuffed lion and an even larger stuffed turtle on Michelle's bed. It was completely covered by her stuffed animal collection.

"So, what gives?" Darcy asked. "Was the team *that* bad?"

"Worse," Stephanie replied. "Actually, I talked to Josh about it today," she went on. "He pretty much said that they're getting worse at every practice."

"I heard that the coach is almost ready to give up on them," Darcy added.

"That's it, then. They just can't win without Bingo," Allie declared.

"No," Stephanie said. "They just *think* they can't."

"But it comes down to the same thing," Darcy pointed out. "If they think they can't win, they won't."

"True," Stephanie agreed. "Listen, guys, about this spy business. I—"

"We know, Steph—you don't have to say anything," Allie told her. "I guess I never really believed you could get Bingo back. It was too much to ask."

"I feel terrible about it," Stephanie answered. It wasn't exactly a lie. She *did* feel terrible. She felt like a complete traitor. She knew she was letting down the entire basketball team. But Bingo should go free. There was no doubt in her mind.

She kept trying to find a way to tell her friends the truth—but how could she? How could they understand?

"Listen, we're really impressed at how hard

you tried, Steph," Allie said. "Let's just not talk about it anymore. Bingo is gone, and that's that." She gazed at the stack of library books on Stephanie's desk. "Wow. Look at all these books on World War Two. They're for your heritage project, aren't they?"

Stephanie nodded.

"Darcy finished hers last night," Allie went on.

"You did?" Stephanie turned to Darcy, feeling relieved to change the subject. "How long is it?" she asked.

"Twelve big ones!" Darcy answered.

"Mine is only ten pages," Allie said. "But I still have some stuff to write. I think I might finish it tonight. How's yours coming, Steph?"

"Not so good," Stephanie admitted. "All I've found is some pretty boring stuff. Jane Tanner worked for forty years as a schoolteacher. She wasn't crazy about my father's salt-shaker–balancing trick. And, oh, yeah, here's the really exciting part—she won a state fair baking contest three years in a row. Peach cobbler pie every time."

"That's pretty dull, all right," Allie agreed.

"Tell me about it!" Stephanie said.

"How many pages have you written?" Darcy asked.

"Two," Stephanie said in a small voice.

"Two?" Darcy's eyes widened. "But, Steph, the paper is due next week! And it's worth a third of our grade."

"I know." Stephanie felt a fresh stab of misery. Nothing was going right.

Allie looked stricken. "Oh, Steph—it's because you spent so much time trying to find Bingo. Now I feel terrible. It was selfish of me to make you do all that spying."

"Selfish?" Stephanie shook her head. "No, I wanted to find Bingo, too. And, to tell you the truth, well, I—"

Bzzzzzzz!

The kitchen timer rang downstairs. "Girls," Stephanie's father called. "I made my special tuna casserole! Who's staying for dinner?"

Darcy crossed her eyes and Allie shuddered.

"Uh—I've got to go," Allie said quickly. "I need to work on my paper tonight."

"I've got to go, too," Darcy said. "I promised to help Allie. Want to do something tomorrow, Steph? Allie and I thought we might go Rollerblading."

"Uh, I can't tomorrow," Stephanie replied. *Be-*

cause tomorrow is the day I set Bingo free. The day I become a total traitor.

"Yeah, I guess you'd better stay home and work on your paper," Allie said, misunderstanding Stephanie's answer.

"Well, call us, okay?" Darcy said. She and Allie waved good-bye as they hurried off.

Stephanie watched her friends escape. It was really impressive how quickly her father's tuna casserole could empty the house. *Maybe they should use it as inspiration for the basketball team,* she thought. *Win the game against Kennedy, or else it's tuna casserole for everyone!*

She grinned at her joke, but it didn't make her feel better.

She went to bed that night with a horrible sick feeling in the pit of her stomach. It was still there when she woke up the next morning.

This is it, she thought. *Today is the day I betray everyone I care about at John Muir.*

She sat up in bed and felt her forehead, hoping for signs of a fever. Nothing. Well, she wouldn't try to get out of it that way. Maybe she could find a different way to help Allie, and Josh, and the John Muir team.

She washed quickly, then stared at her closet. What did you wear to free a raccoon anyway?

Finally she decided on a baseball cap, one of D.J.'s big, bulky sweaters, and dark sunglasses. She stuffed her hair under the cap and put on the shades. It wasn't exactly a foolproof disguise. But it might help in case she ran into someone from John Muir.

Okay, she told her reflection in the mirror. *Ready for Operation Raccoon Release!*

At nine A.M. sharp Stephanie met Dana, Sherri, and Laura inside the main entrance to Golden Gate Park. Dana carried Bingo in a cat carrier.

"Hey, Bingo," Stephanie said when she saw the raccoon. He poked one paw through the wire door and played with the cage. It looked like he was trying to free himself.

"Okay." Dana spread a map of the park out on the ground. "He'll have a good chance to survive if we release him in one of the wilder areas of the park."

Sherri pointed to the map. "This area is perfect. It's got lots of trees," she said. "I think he'd be really happy there."

Dana turned to the cage on the ground and held out her hand. Bingo shoved his black nose against the cage door and sniffed her finger. Dana looked very sad.

"I didn't think this was going to be so hard," she said.

Laura put her hand on Dana's shoulder. "Just think of how happy he'll be when he's free."

Dana reached through the wire door and scratched Bingo's ear. "We'll miss you, little guy," she said.

"Let's just do it," Sherri told her. "Before we all start to cry."

Dana nodded. She stood up, lifting Bingo's cage.

"Bingo!" a voice exclaimed. "It's you!"

Stephanie froze at the sound. "Oh, no!" she muttered.

"What's wrong, Jane?" Laura asked.

Stephanie didn't answer. Her mind was spinning—and so was her stomach. She knew that voice, and when she turned to see where it came from, she realized her worst fear was coming true. Allie and Darcy were Rollerblading right toward her!

CHAPTER
14

◆ ◄ ◆ ◆

Allie and Darcy skated to a quick stop. "Stephanie! You found Bingo!" Allie squealed. "But when? How?"

"Uh, well, yeah. But I—" Stephanie began to explain. She racked her brain for another story, but she drew a total blank. She just stared helplessly from one group of girls to the other.

"Steph?" Allie blinked in confusion. "Who are these girls? What are they doing with Bingo?"

Darcy took a step closer to Dana and her friends. "I've never seen you around John Muir," she said.

Laura stepped forward. "No, you haven't, because we're from Kennedy."

"That's Laura," Sherri said, "and this is Dana, and I'm Sherri."

Darcy stared at them. "You're from Kennedy?"

"That's right," Dana replied in a friendly tone. "And we're just about to let Bingo go."

"We found the perfect spot in the woods. He'll be very safe there," Sherri added.

"You can't release him!" Allie's eyes widened in horror. She turned to Stephanie. "We got here just in time. You were going to stop them, weren't you?"

"No, Allie. Actually, I—" Stephanie said.

"Why would she stop us?" Dana demanded.

Darcy stared at Stephanie in disbelief. "You were going to help set him free? You were helping them?"

Stephanie swallowed. "It's not like you think. Let's all just talk about this calmly, and—"

Darcy slowly shook her head. "I never even guessed. I bet you knew where Bingo was all along, didn't you?"

"Not all along," Stephanie replied.

Allie gaped at her. "It can't be true. Stephanie, tell me it isn't true!"

"Stephanie?" Dana repeated. "I thought your name was Jane Calzo."

"Well, it's not," Darcy said. "Her *real* name is

Stephanie Tanner, and she goes to John Muir. And the only reason she was friends with you was that she was spying on you. She was supposed to find Bingo.''

''And she did,'' Allie said. ''But obviously, she's gone over to your side now.''

''Allie, you know that's not true,'' Stephanie tried to explain. ''I never—''

''You know our team can't win without Bingo,'' Allie argued. ''How could you do this? You—you traitor!''

''Wait a minute. Are they telling the truth?'' Dana asked Stephanie. She looked totally hurt. ''Did you really spy on us? And lie to us?''

''I—uh, it started out that way, but—'' Stephanie began.

''I can't believe it!'' Dana cut her off. ''We felt bad because you were the new kid. We went out of our way to help you fit in—to be your friends. And you were using us! I feel so stupid!''

''Not as stupid as I feel,'' another voice added.

Stephanie whirled. ''Billy!'' she exclaimed.

Billy leaned down to pat a German shepherd who stood quietly on his leash. Stephanie groaned. Why did Billy have to choose this morning to walk his dog in the park?

Billy shook his head, looking as if she'd just hit him. "I thought you really liked me," he said.

"I *did* like you," Stephanie insisted. "I mean, I *do* like you!"

"You don't even go to Kennedy," Billy went on. "You lied to me, too!"

"I didn't want to," Stephanie said. "You don't understand. It's very complicated!"

"No, it isn't. It's very simple. You aren't Jane. Your family didn't go to San Diego," Billy said. "And you didn't get a cold from your sister. Those were all lies." His mouth set in a thin line. "I can't believe I actually felt badly for you because your great-aunt died!"

"Stop arguing about it!" Allie stooped down next to Bingo's cage. "Bingo is the one who matters."

"I agree," Dana told her. "That's why we're letting him go."

"But you had no right to take him," Allie declared. "I'm the one who took him in when his foot was injured," she reminded them.

"That doesn't mean he has to live out his life in a cage," Dana shot back. "Saving him doesn't give you the right to keep him in prison."

"Hey—what's up?" a male voice called.

Stephanie looked up and groaned out loud.

Josh, Rob, and Eric Haas, another John Muir basketball player, were heading their way, dribbling a basketball.

Allie spun around. "Over here," she called out, waving to them. "Hurry!"

Josh's eyes lit up with excitement when he spotted the cage on the ground. "Guys, look! It's Bingo! They found him." The boys ran up. Josh and Eric slapped a high-five.

"Hooray!" Eric cheered. "Our luck has turned!"

"Kennedy will lose, big time!" Rob yelled.

Josh whooped and thrust his fist into the air. "Bingo is back! Raccoons rule!" he shouted.

Stephanie turned to Billy with a smile of apology. "They play for our team," she explained.

"No kidding," Billy answered. He stared coldly at her. "I've got to hand it to you," he said. "You are one amazing liar." He tugged on his dog's leash. "Let's go, Jackson," he said.

"Billy, wait," Stephanie said. Billy walked away.

She watched him go, feeling totally helpless. *Do something. Say something!* she told herself. *Billy is special. Don't just let him go, thinking that you're a liar! Tell him that—*

Allie's voice interrupted her thoughts.

"Wait, you guys. Stephanie *did* find Bingo," Allie told the boys. "But she was about to help the Kennedy kids set him free."

"What?" Josh's eyes widened in disbelief.

"It's true, Josh," Stephanie said. "Because it's the right thing to do."

"You'd do that to our team mascot? Why?" Josh demanded.

"Because it's cruel to keep a wild animal in a cage," Dana replied before Stephanie could answer.

"We would never be cruel to Bingo," Allie declared. "I love Bingo more than anyone does! More than any of you."

"Oh, really?" Dana demanded. She turned to Stephanie. "Well, Jane—or Stephanie, or whoever you are," she sputtered, "I don't blame you for tricking these bozos. What is their problem anyway?" she asked. "Do they really think having a raccoon at the game is what makes them win?"

"Absolutely," Eric said.

"Without a doubt," Josh told her.

"No question," Rob agreed.

"You sound like superstitious morons," Sherri told them.

"Really, you guys—they have a point," Stephanie tried to say. "If you'd just listen to Dana. All she cares about is doing what's best for Bingo. Animals have rights, too, you know."

"Listen, you're all forgetting one very important thing," Allie said in a tone of voice Stephanie had never heard before.

"Bingo was in a John Muir biology lab," Allie went on. "And some of you Kennedy kids broke in and stole him. Our biology teacher called the police to report him stolen. All I have to do is tell them we found the thieves—and you'll all be in major trouble."

Dana and Sherri exchanged a look of panic.

"But we won't call the police if you give us Bingo," Allie finished.

"That's blackmail!" Laura protested.

"Yes, but you deserve it. You stole our raccoon," Darcy reminded her.

Dana shook her head sadly. "He was never *yours*," she said. "No one can own a wild animal. I hope you realize that someday."

"I guess some people think only of themselves," Sherri muttered.

Allie reached down and grabbed Bingo's cage. She glared at Dana, Sherri, and Laura. She turned her back on them. "Come on, Darcy," she said. "Let's get Bingo back to John Muir."

"All right!" Darcy exclaimed. Josh slapped Eric and Rob on the back. They turned to follow Allie out of the park.

"Allie, wait! Darcy—listen to me," Stephanie called out.

Allie kept going. Darcy hesitated for a moment. Her dark eyes searched Stephanie's. "I'm sorry, Steph," she finally said. "But your *real* friends and your *real* school should have come first. You totally let us down." She skated after Allie.

Stephanie watched them go. She had never felt so totally alone before.

Way to go, Stephanie, she told herself. *You just lost your two best friends in the world.*

"Great. Nice work, whoever you are," Dana said to Stephanie. She folded her arms over her chest. Her blue eyes blazed with anger. "You set this up perfectly. You told them exactly where we'd be today, didn't you?"

"No, I wouldn't do that," Stephanie protested. "I thought you were right. I thought Bingo should be released. That's why I came to help you. I had no idea they would be here this morning. It was a total coincidence!"

Sherri gave a bitter laugh. "Right," she said. "Your two best friends, plus half the John Muir basketball team? Some coincidence. You really expect us to believe that?"

Stephanie had to admit it sounded totally lame.

"Let's go," Dana said. "She got what she wanted. It's just a shame that Bingo has to pay for it." Dana marched off. Sherri and Laura hurried after her.

Stephanie dragged herself home. She had tried so hard to do the right thing. How had it all turned out so badly?

She unlocked the front door and headed into the living room. Her father was sitting on the couch, reading the paper.

He looked up as soon as he saw her. "Hi, Steph," he said. "I'm glad you're home. I have something important to tell you."

"But what are you doing here?" Stephanie asked. "I thought everyone but me was going on a picnic today."

"The rest of the family went," Danny replied. "But I had something special to do." He peered closely at her. "You look upset," he said. "Is anything wrong?"

Stephanie was about to say "nothing." But she couldn't bring herself to tell another lie. "Everything!" she blurted out instead.

The whole horrible story came pouring out. She explained how she'd decided to find Bingo all on her own by becoming a spy—just like Great-Aunt Jane. She described how she became friends with the Kennedy kids, and how she found Bingo. She explained how she realized that she agreed with Dana. And finally she told her dad about that morning's mission to free the raccoon.

"Now Darcy and Allie and Josh are furious at me. And so are Dana and Billy and their friends. I guess I didn't inherit Great-Aunt Jane's spying skills after all. I've wrecked my entire social life. Plus an innocent little raccoon is stuck in a cage forever," she finished.

Danny gave her a strange look. He acted almost embarrassed about something. "That sounds pretty terrible," he agreed. "I'm just sorry you thought you had to be like Great-Aunt Jane."

"I know," Stephanie replied. "I could never be a great spy like her."

"That's what I wanted to tell you about." Danny paused. "You're not the only one who was fascinated by the idea of a spy in the family. I was so curious that I did a little research on my own, and I found something—very surprising."

Danny lifted a section of the newspaper he was reading. He handed it to her, pointing out a photograph.

"Hey—this is the same photograph of Great-Aunt Jane!" Stephanie exclaimed. She glanced at the date on the top of the page: October 31, 1940. "Where did you find this?" she asked.

Her father smiled. "In a box in the attic," he told her. "It was stuck in a box with my insect collection, from when I was nine."

"Yuck," Stephanie said. "No wonder I didn't go near it."

"Go ahead and read the article that goes with Aunt Jane's photo," Danny told her.

Stephanie quickly scanned it. "But this is the local society page," she said in confusion. "All they ever talk about are parties and weddings. What do spies have to do with that kind of thing?"

"Finish the article and you'll see." Danny pointed lower down on the page.

Stephanie read it through. "Oh, no," she murmured. She glanced up at her father in disbelief. "How can this be?"

CHAPTER
15

◆ ◀ ◗ ◆

"This means—" Stephanie was afraid to finish her thought.

Danny nodded. "I'm afraid it's true, Steph. Great-Aunt Jane was famous—for throwing huge Halloween parties. They were the highlight of San Francisco's fall social season."

Stephanie stared at the photograph in dismay. "And this is a picture of Great-Aunt Jane in her Halloween costume. Her *spy* costume," Stephanie groaned. "No wonder I failed. The Tanners don't have spying in their blood. They have Halloween parties."

"It takes talent to throw a good party," Danny told her.

"Oh, Dad. This is a *double* disaster!" Stephanie wailed. "Not only have I lost all my friends. But now I'm stuck with no subject for my heritage project! And it's due this Friday!"

"Actually, that's not true. You still have something interesting to write about," her father told her. "It turns out that Jane did more than throw parties."

"She did?" Stephanie asked.

"You bet. Jane Tanner was quite a traveler. I also found one of her travel diaries in that box. And souvenirs and more photographs."

Danny showed Stephanie a stack of postcards and photographs from the American West.

"It seems Aunt Jane had an interest in Native American culture," Danny continued. "She traveled all over the West, visiting different Indian peoples. And then she set up exchange programs between the kids in her school and the kids on the reservations."

"Really?" Stephanie asked. "That *is* pretty cool."

"I think you're going to have a great report after all," Danny said.

Stephanie smiled with relief. "I'm glad one part of my life is fixed. Now, if only you could straighten out the mess with Bingo," she said.

"You know, even though things are in bad shape right now, I'm really proud of you," Danny told her.

"You are?" Stephanie asked. "You're proud that I lied to my new friends and betrayed my old ones?" Stephanie stared at her father to see if he was teasing.

Danny chuckled. "I'm proud that you were able to see both sides of the story," he told her. "You didn't let your loyalty to Allie, and Josh, and John Muir blind you to Dana's arguments."

"Yeah, but where does seeing both sides get me?" Stephanie demanded.

"Actually," her father said, "I think it's gotten you into a unique position. You're the perfect person to help everyone reach a compromise. An agreement where both sides are happy."

Stephanie looked doubtful. "How? I'd have to come up with a plan where John Muir gets to keep its mascot—and the Kennedy kids get to set him free."

"I know it sounds impossible," Danny told her. "But I have faith in you, Steph. You're creative. I'm sure you'll come up with something."

"I'm not so sure," Stephanie muttered.

"Well, don't decide anything right now," her

dad told her. "Let's just go take a look at Aunt Jane's diary. Okay?"

"Okay," Stephanie replied. "I sure don't have anything better to do."

The next week at school for Stephanie was totally miserable. She tried to apologize to Allie and Darcy and Josh. She even tried to tell the basketball team that she was sorry. But no one would speak to her. No one would listen.

She walked to school alone and ate lunch alone. No one wanted her on their team in gym class. Most kids acted as if she simply didn't exist.

By Wednesday she was ready to scream. *At least I have a meeting for* The Scribe *today,* she thought. *They'll have to talk to me at a newspaper meeting.* She was so excited about it that she nearly ran all the way to the media center.

Sue Kramer, the editor of the paper, met her outside the door. Sue was always friendly to Stephanie.

"Hi, Sue!" Stephanie was never so glad to see her before.

"Wait, Stephanie. You don't want to go in there," Sue replied before Stephanie could enter the room. She handed Stephanie an envelope.

"What's this?" Stephanie asked.

"Your next writing assignment," Sue told her. "It's probably better if you don't come to this meeting. Some kids are afraid you might tell our secrets to the staff of the Kennedy paper."

"I would never do that," Stephanie protested.

"Well, I know that, but lots of kids are really upset. I mean, you were going to help Kennedy release Bingo," Sue reminded her.

Stephanie stared at the envelope. "Do you think I was wrong?" she asked Sue.

"I don't know," Sue said. "I guess I can see both sides of the story."

"Just like me," Stephanie muttered. "Anyway, thanks for giving me another assignment," she told Sue. "It means a lot to me."

"Good luck," Sue told her.

Stephanie shoved the envelope into her backpack and went home. As soon as she got to her room she sat down and wrote two notes, one to Dana and another one to Billy. She told them both how sorry she was about everything that had happened. She asked them each to call so they could talk things over.

The last two days of the week dragged on. Stephanie finished her heritage report on Thursday, in time to hand it in the next day.

Well, Dad was right about one thing, she thought. *I did write a really interesting paper about Great-Aunt Jane after all.*

Still, she hadn't come up with a compromise to make everyone happy. Not that it mattered. No one was talking to her anyway. Allie wouldn't speak, and Darcy would nod hello or good-bye. Neither Dana nor Billy answered her letters.

Friday afternoon she stood in front of her locker, feeling as if she couldn't face one more minute of the silent treatment. Thank goodness school was over for the week!

Two eighth-grade girls ran past, chatting excitedly about the big pep rally.

I can't believe it! I forgot about the rally, Stephanie realized.

The big game with Kennedy was the next day, and the outdoor pep rally was about to begin. *I should go,* she thought. *I still care about John Muir. I still want the team to win.*

Allie and Darcy would be there. They'd probably just ignore her. *But what if they call me a traitor in front of everybody?* she worried.

Stephanie suddenly felt a burst of anger. *But I'm not a traitor,* she told herself. *I want John Muir to win the game. In fact, I went to a lot of trouble so they would win. The only thing I'm really guilty of is that I saw both sides of the problem—and I tried to help everyone. That's nothing to be ashamed of.*

Stephanie took a deep breath. Then she threw her books into her locker. She grabbed her denim jacket and headed outside for the pep rally. Loud cheers rang out as she pushed through the front doors. She paused on the top step. The cheers were getting louder. Only they didn't sound exactly right.

Stephanie hurried down the steps. The John Muir cheerleaders stood on a platform, cheering, "We're number one! We're number one!" The basketball team cheered along. So did the rest of the John Muir students.

But they were surrounded by a circle of kids from Kennedy. The Kennedy kids held signs and were shouting back: "Hey, John Muir, what do you know? Your caged raccoon has got to go! Free Bingo! Free Bingo! Free Bingo!"

Stephanie recognized Dana leading the group. Sherri and Laura and Billy were there, too. So were most of the Kennedy basketball team.

Some of the basketball players broke away from the pep rally and started toward the group from Kennedy. They did not look friendly. "Fight! Fight!" some kids in the crowd chanted.

Stephanie frowned. Someone had to stop this before it got out of hand. And she was the only one there who knew the Kennedy kids.

Stephanie marched up to Dana and her friends. "Just calm everyone down," she told them. "Let's talk this over."

"Why should we listen to you?" Laura demanded.

"Yeah, Jane," Billy added. "I mean, Stephanie. Or is it Wanda today? Or Maggie?"

"That's not fair," Stephanie said.

"Whatever you say, Jane." Billy turned his back on her.

Stephanie pushed through the Kennedy crowd and started toward the John Muir group. But Josh and his friends stepped out of the crowd and blocked her way.

"You don't really belong here," he said.

"Of course I do. I happen to care about John Muir," Stephanie replied.

"You sure didn't act that way," Josh replied.

"Yeah. You belong with our enemy," Rob added.

"I do *not!*" Stephanie protested.

Stephanie felt her temper skyrocket. "All right, that's it," she shouted. "I've had it with all of you! You are all totally, completely wrong!

About me and one another. But especially about Bingo!"

There was a short silence. Then Allie stepped forward. Darcy was at her side.

"What do you mean?" Allie said. They were the first words she had spoken to Stephanie all week.

Stephanie took a deep breath. *All right, this is it. This is your big chance to get everyone together,* she told herself. *And you'd better not blow it!*

CHAPTER
16

◆ ◀ ◢ ◆

Stephanie faced Allie, trying to speak calmly. "To start with, the kids at Kennedy are not our enemies," she said. "They're kids—just like us. They care about their school and they care about one another. And they want to win this basketball game."

"Which is why they stole Bingo," Allie retorted.

"No!" Stephanie said. "You're wrong. That had *nothing* to do with the game."

"She's right," Dana announced to the crowd. "The reason my friends and I took Bingo had nothing to do with your basketball game. We just wanted to make sure he didn't spend his life in a cage! How would you like it if *you* were locked up?"

Stephanie turned to Allie and Darcy. "Remember when Bingo first came to John Muir? We said we'd release him as soon as his foot was healed. Remember, Allie? I know you love Bingo. And you want to keep him around. But you're breaking your promise to him. And that's not fair."

Allie bit her lip. Stephanie could see she was thinking about what she said.

Josh was gazing at Stephanie as though she were insane. "Bingo is our mascot," he protested. "We can't let him go now!"

"We need a raccoon there to cheer us on," Rob added. "Otherwise we'll lose the game!"

Cheer us on? Yes! That's it! Stephanie grinned. *That could really work.*

"Not if we compromise," Stephanie told Rob and Josh. "And I just came up with the way to do it. It's a perfect plan."

"Why should we listen to it?" Rob demanded.

"Because you *do* care about Bingo," Stephanie said. "Because deep down we all know what's right for him. We know we have to let him go sometime."

"But not now!" Allie exclaimed. She gave Stephanie a pleading look.

"I'm sorry, Al," Stephanie said in a low voice. "I know how much you love him. But you have to let him go. He belongs in the wild."

"I know," Allie muttered.

"Listen, everybody!" Stephanie announced. "I have an idea for a compromise. It should make everybody happy."

"Kennedy *and* John Muir?" Darcy asked. She looked doubtful.

"It's true, Darce," Stephanie said. "Believe me. But you have to be willing to hear me out. Are you?"

"I am," Dana declared. Sherri and Laura exchanged a curious look, then nodded.

Josh seemed a little embarrassed. "Hey, if Kennedy is willing to listen, I guess I am, too," he said.

Darcy turned to Allie. "Maybe we should listen to her, Al," she said. "I mean, we *did* get a little carried away."

Allie slowly nodded. "I guess we should."

Stephanie felt like cheering out loud. Instead, she took a deep breath.

"Okay," Stephanie began. "I think we all agree on one thing—Bingo deserves to go free. Very soon. But the John Muir kids took care of Bingo while his foot was hurt. I think we should get to keep him for one more day. So why not let Bingo go to one last game? And afterward we could all go to the park together. We'll all set him free. With the help of the Urban Park Rangers," she added.

A low murmur of approval swept through the crowd.

"Sounds fair to me," Josh declared. "As long as Bingo's at the game."

"I guess it does make sense," Allie replied.

"I agree," Dana said.

"Great!" Stephanie beamed.

"But what's the rest of the compromise?" Darcy asked.

Stephanie grinned. "It's something that will let us have Bingo—even when we *don't* have him."

"Huh? I don't get it," Josh said.

"You'll see at the game. Trust me," Stephanie said. She nodded toward the cheerleaders. "But right now we have a pep rally to finish!"

There was a moment of silence. Then the cheerleaders lifted their pom-poms high in the air. "We're number one!" they shouted.

The John Muir crowd picked up the chant. The Kennedy kids spoke quietly to each other for a minute. Then they drifted away.

Dana and her friends left Stephanie standing with Allie and Darcy.

"Steph, I—" Allie started to say.

"You know I never—" Darcy said.

"You guys, I was so—" Stephanie blurted out.

They all looked at one another and burst out laughing.

"I guess we're all sorry—for all the bad stuff that happened between us," Allie finally said.

"And I hope we never, ever fight like this again," Darcy added.

"Me, too," Stephanie agreed. She and Allie gave each other a huge hug.

Darcy flung an arm around Stephanie's shoulders. "It took a lot of guts to stand up to that crowd," Darcy said.

"Totally!" Allie agreed.

"Actually, I'm really glad it's over," Stephanie told them. "I never want to go undercover again!"

"Hey—how about pizza at Tony's?" Darcy suggested. "To celebrate being friends again."

"Sounds great." Stephanie dug through her backpack for a quarter. "Wait for me while I phone my dad. I need to tell him I'll be late."

Stephanie rushed around the corner of the school, heading for the pay phone. "Billy!" She gaped at him in surprise. "What are you doing here? Didn't everyone go back to Kennedy?"

"Yeah," Billy answered. "But I was hoping I'd catch you if I waited around. Can you talk for a minute?"

"Sure," Stephanie replied. She noticed that the sunlight made his brown hair an incredible shade of reddish gold. She had a feeling that if he took off his glasses, he'd be even cuter.

Stephanie hesitated. "I really am sorry I lied to you," she finally said. "Actually, I wanted to go out with you. But I didn't know how to handle it. I mean, I knew you'd find out there was no Jane Calzo, and—"

"And that would be hard to explain," Billy agreed. "But I'm sorry for some of the things I said to you, too." He scratched his head, as if unsure of what to say next. "You know, I learned a little bit about Jane Calzo. But I know next to nothing about Stephanie Tanner."

"So maybe we could spend some time getting to know each other," Stephanie suggested.

"Great idea!" Billy beamed at her.

"Why don't you meet me after the game tomorrow?" Stephanie asked.

"Is that a good idea?" Billy frowned. "What if Kennedy beats you?"

"I'll still want to meet you, Billy," Stephanie replied. "Remember? We both think this rivalry thing is silly. And besides"—her eyes twinkled—"I'll want to hear what you think after you see my great compromise plan—part two."

Billy looked puzzled. "What is it exactly?"

"It's still a secret," Stephanie replied. "But you'll see what it is tomorrow—at the game!"

CHAPTER
17

◆ ◀ ◆ ◆

Stephanie glanced at the clock on the wall of the John Muir girls' locker room. "Ten minutes till game time," she murmured.

She checked her reflection in the mirror, then turned to Darcy and Allie. "How do I look?" she asked.

"Different." Darcy giggled.

"Do you think the school is really ready for this?" Stephanie asked.

"Absolutely," Darcy assured her. "You came up with the perfect plan, Steph. The team will flip out when they see their new mascot."

"And we're still set to release the real Bingo after the game," Allie reminded them.

"And I'm set to meet Billy," Stephanie added. "So everyone will be happy!"

Allie made a few adjustments to Stephanie's outfit.

Darcy dug a large furry object out of a box. "Ready for your head?" she asked.

"Ready," Stephanie replied.

Darcy lowered a giant raccoon head over Stephanie's face. The furry mask rested on her shoulders. Darcy fastened the head to the thick white collar that circled Stephanie's neck. She straightened the tag that hung from the collar. The name BINGO was spelled out across the tag in big black letters.

"Are you okay in there?" Allie asked.

"It's hot. And awfully dark," Stephanie said.

"Just a minute. I'll fix that." Darcy twisted the head until Stephanie could see through the two eyeholes.

"Well," Stephanie said. "At least now I can see."

Stephanie twirled in front of the mirror. "How do I look?"

Allie and Darcy grinned at her. "You look great, 'Bingo!' Ready to go?"

"As ready as I'll ever be!" Stephanie replied.

Moments later she stepped onto the basket-ball court.

A giant cheer—and shouts of laughter—rang out from the crowd. Even the Kennedy kids were clapping!

"Way to go, Bingo," the cheerleaders began to chant. The crowd took up the cry. "Way to go, Bingo! Way to go, Bingo!"

Stephanie skipped across the floor. Josh ran out in his uniform and bounced the basketball her way. She caught it and threw a few foul shots. The last one sank into the basket.

A roar of approval surged through the crowd.

Stephanie ran to center court and turned a cartwheel. The entire gym rose to its feet, clapping and cheering.

Mr. Thompson, John Muir's principal, hurried onto the gym floor. "Thank you, Bingo!" he called through a microphone. "It's game time now. But I hope you come back during halftime!"

Stephanie nodded and saluted Mr. Thompson. Then she gave him a low bow and danced off the court, waving to the crowd. More cheers and applause followed her into the hall outside the locker rooms. Darcy and Allie were waiting for her.

"Steph—I mean, Bingo—you were great!" Allie exclaimed.

Darcy helped Stephanie pull off the raccoon head. Just then her dad appeared in the hallway. "The crowd loved you!" he cried.

Stephanie wiped a bead of sweat off her forehead. "Thanks for finding this costume for us, Dad. But I'm glad I won't have to wear it at every game," she added.

"So Mr. Thompson and the coach agreed?" Danny asked.

"That's right," Stephanie told him. "Kids will take turns being Bingo—a different kid for each game."

"Hold it right there!" a boy shouted. Stephanie recognized an eighth-grader who took photographs for *The Scribe*.

He aimed his camera at her, and a flash went off. "Thanks!" he called. Stephanie couldn't help laughing.

"What's so funny?" Danny asked.

"Oh," Stephanie said, "I just wondered if one of my descendants will see that photograph someday. They could spend weeks trying to write a report about their great-aunt Stephanie. The famous spy who went undercover—as a raccoon!"

It doesn't matter if you live around the corner...
or around the world...
If you are a fan of Mary-Kate and Ashley Olsen,
you should be a member of

MARY–KATE + ASHLEY'S FUN CLUB™

Here's what you get:
Our Funzine™
An autographed color photo
Two black & white individual photos
A full size color poster
An official **Fun Club™** membership card
A **Fun Club™** school folder
Two special **Fun Club™** surprises
A holiday card
Fun Club™ collectibles catalog
Plus a **Fun Club™** box to keep everything in

To join Mary-Kate + Ashley's Fun Club™, fill out the form
below and send it along with

U.S. Residents – $17.00
Canadian Residents – $22 U.S. Funds
International Residents – $27 U.S. Funds

MARY-KATE + ASHLEY'S FUN CLUB™
859 HOLLYWOOD WAY, SUITE 275
BURBANK, CA 91505

NAME:_____

ADDRESS:_____

_CITY:_____ STATE:_____ ZIP:_____

PHONE:(____) _____ BIRTHDATE:_____

1242

FULL HOUSE™
Michelle

#5: THE GHOST IN MY CLOSET 53573-0/$3.99

#6: BALLET SURPRISE 53574-9/$3.99

#7: MAJOR LEAGUE TROUBLE 53575-7/$3.99

#8: MY FOURTH-GRADE MESS 53576-5/$3.99

#9: BUNK 3, TEDDY, AND ME 56834-5/$3.99

#10: MY BEST FRIEND IS A MOVIE STAR!
(Super Edition) 56835-3/$3.99

#11: THE BIG TURKEY ESCAPE 56836-1/$3.99

#12: THE SUBSTITUTE TEACHER 00364-X/$3.99

#13: CALLING ALL PLANETS 00365-8/$3.99

#14: I'VE GOT A SECRET 00366-6/$3.99

#15: HOW TO BE COOL 00833-1/$3.99

#16: THE NOT-SO-GREAT OUTDOORS 00835-8/$3.99

#17: MY HO-HO-HORRIBLE CHRISTMAS 00836-6/$3.99

MY AWESOME HOLIDAY FRIENDSHIP BOOK
(An Activity Book) 00840-4/$3.99

FULL HOUSE MICHELLE OMNIBUS 02181-8/$6.99

#18: MY ALMOST PERFECT PLAN 00837-4/$3.99

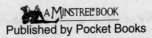
A MINSTREL® BOOK
Published by Pocket Books

Simon & Schuster Mail Order Dept. BWB
200 Old Tappan Rd., Old Tappan, N.J. 07675

Please send me the books I have checked above. I am enclosing $_____ (please add $0.75 to cover the
postage and handling for each order. Please add appropriate sales tax). Send check or money order--no cash or C.O.D.'s please. Allow up to
six weeks for delivery. For purchase over $10.00 you may use VISA: card number, expiration date and customer signature must be included.

Name _____

Address _____

City _____ State/Zip _____

VISA Card # _____ Exp.Date _____

Signature _____

1033-25

FULL HOUSE Stephanie™

Available from Minstrel® Books Published by Pocket Books